Jarred Dreams

Camilla.

CAMILLA CHESTER

Matador
9 Priory Business Park,
Wistow Road, Kibworth Beauchamp,
Leicestershire. LE8 0RX
Tel: 0116 279 2299
Email: books@troubador.co.uk
Web: www.troubador.co.uk/matador
Twitter: @matadorbooks

ISBN 978 1785892 394

British Library Cataloguing in Publication Data.
A catalogue record for this book is available from the British Library.

Printed and bound by CPI Group (UK) Ltd, Croydon, CR0 4YY
Typeset in Aldine401 BT by Troubador Publishing Ltd, Leicester, UK

Matador is an imprint of Troubador Publishing Ltd

For Fay and Sasha

CHAPTER ONE

Dream Thief

The Dream Thief taps a curled black nail on the glass of the jar. He can see through his almost translucent hand as the dream twitches in response. Flurries of pale-green sparks dart diagonally out from the dream's core, rebound against its prison and fold back in on it. An ancient label flutters from the jar's surface, landing carelessly on the floor. It is illuminated by the colourful magic from the jars. He reads it:

TRUDY DADE
AGE 6: PUPPETEER DANCE IN ICING
SUGAR GARDENS

He looks at the yellowed paper but has no memory of making the label or stealing the dream. He wonders for a moment about the warmth it may have given him. Other labels lie with it on the cellar floor. Feeling no need to read them, instead he turns away from the jarred dreams, disappointed by their unfulfilled promises, blind to their beauty.

The Dream Thief shuffles to the hat stand, roughly

grabs his black pull-string bag, releasing it from the hook and opens it. He has packed the things he will need: his dry, ashy food, a flask of water, a child-sized blanket on which to sleep. It's two days, three at most, so he can afford to travel light, and the going will be easier once he is out of The Grey.

His bag in order, he hoists it onto his back, adjusting the strings over his shoulders. He reaches for his cloak from the hat stand and throws it over his head and hunched shoulders like a shroud. His ears stick up; so pointed and alert they almost poke through the fabric of his hood. He looks around for an empty jar, but all he sees are dancing lights. The shelves are full of jars, none of them empty. It seems unbelievable, yet it's always so far from being over. Taking one of the few remaining empty jars that he spots on one of the bottom shelves, he ties it to his belt loop under his cloak.

Before he leaves he looks at the only jar that's half empty and a throaty snort of disgust or perhaps disappointment, escapes his thin lips. It stands at the front, apart from the hundreds of other dreams. He approaches it, but is distracted by his reflection against the glass. The skin on his face is a sickly yellow and it deters him from watching the dream. He looks instead at his deep-set, hooded black eyes, his large, hooked, nose and his pointed chin. His reflection moves eerily across the surface of the jar, like smoke. He decides against watching the first dream and instead he leaves quickly by the coal chute as usual.

It's night, which is usually the best time, and he

sniffs a little, dog-like, at the damp air. He knows the dream he wants and he steps out onto the endless grey pavements of Stanbridge, into the permanent drizzle, to take it; hoping, as always, that it will feel as good as the first.

That first dream gave him a feeling he can never repeat no matter how many more dreams he steals. Yet he will go on because he's the Dream Thief. To rid the world of dreams is his cause and there is nobody who has the power to stop him.

CHAPTER TWO

Sade

Sade is in the front passenger seat beside her dad as they drive down the motorway. The space between and behind them is packed with all their possessions. They hardly speak; there are lots of things that Sade wants to say, but it's difficult to know how to start. Her dad's hand rests on the gear stick, the gold of his wedding band glinting slightly and Sade thinks about the matching one on her mum Elspeth's hand. She opens her mouth to say something, but shuts it again, turning and looking out of the window instead. She shifts her gaze beyond her reflection of freckled skin, bright, intense blue eyes and shock of blonde curls to the outside and watches as they turn off from the stream of fast traffic.

The journey is a familiar one and she knows that it won't be long before she sees Stanbridge Hospital, the strange clunky building that houses her sleeping mum. She likes to think of her as simply sleeping; coma is too much of a scary word. This time is different though. This time they will drive past the hospital and on into the town. Sade has never been into Stanbridge itself, but she's known for a week that they are moving to be nearer her mum.

'I'm sorry, Sah,' her dad had said to her, 'sorry that I'm making you grow up more quickly than you should.'

Sade had looked at her dad's broad forehead, noticing the way his eyebrows furrowed when he said something important and she felt a pang for the past when loving her mum and dad was a simple thing to do.

'Twelve is old enough, Dad,' she'd said and she'd meant it. 'It's all good; we can move.'

The sky darkens the further they drive towards Stanbridge. Sade manages to wriggle an arm free to check her watch. It's only three thirty; she wonders if a storm is on the way.

'I hope it doesn't rain,' she says to her dad. 'That will make shifting the stuff in a right pain.'

'Yeah,' agrees her dad, 'looks like it's just a bit of drizzle though. We can cope with drizzle.'

They drive past the hospital and into the town. She looks out, trying to spot some school kids, but there's nobody about at all. Yesterday, her last day of school, was horrible. She had to leave behind all her friends and she'd cried. She keeps scanning. Surely kids would be coming out of school about now? Then she sees a girl, walking alone. She's wearing a thick, heavy-looking, steel-grey uniform, with a crested blazer and matching satchel worn across her shoulder. She walks straight-backed, almost as if she's marching. Poor girl, thinks Sade, she must be the unpopular one.

Sade tries to get a good look at the girl's face so that she can make sure she's nice to her on Monday, but it's hidden, or is it just expressionless? Either way Sade knows she will never remember her again.

Then she sees another school kid, of about her own age, a boy this time, again dressed in the uniform of her new school, Stanbridge High. Like the girl, he walks alone, straight-backed, satchel across his shoulder. Then here's another walking alone, and another.

'Look, there's some kids from your new school. Smart uniform eh?'

'Bit dismal. Like something out of the army. Why aren't they talking? They're all walking on their own.'

'Oh yeah! Don't ask me, kids are weird.'

'Cheers.'

Her dad laughs a little. 'Here we are, thirty-one Camberley Street, Stanbridge, our new home,' he says, parking the car up next to the kerb.

Sade looks up at the house. It's one of a long line: boxy, nondescript and exactly the same as all the others on the street. She checks her wing-mirror before she opens the door to the car, but there's no sign of any traffic. Then she realises that she has not seen a single car since arriving in the town.

She opens the door and swings out her legs; it feels good to stretch them out after having them curled uncomfortably around all the breakables. She manages to rock herself up and carries the box that has been perched on her knee, obscuring her view, over the damp paving slabs that turn from pavement into garden path without any change in definition.

The house is a little cold, with a slight fusty, un-lived in, damp smell. Sade puts the box down on the charcoal carpet in the front room.

'The removers have already been and gone, that's good isn't it?' says her dad, running his hand over the back of the settee that looks lost and out of place in its new home.

Sade says nothing and instead sets to work unpacking the car. As she steps back outside she sees the house opposite. It stands out of the smart, tidy row like a bad tooth. The house is so dark it's almost black, in contrast to the standard grey of all its neighbours. Its upstairs windows are boarded up and there's what looks like scorch marks disfiguring the brick. Sade looks around for her dad to comment on it, but there's nobody about. Even the single-file children seem to have disappeared from sight. She shudders a little, even though it's not cold, opens the boot and starts unloading.

'Shall we go take a look around town?' suggests Sade later. They sit on the sofa, surrounded by labelled boxes, sipping tea.

'We should really visit Mum.'

Sade checks her watch. 'Visiting isn't until six, so we have an hour. Quick walk round town? Find out where school is, say hello to a few locals, that kind of thing?'

Her dad smiles and sips his tea. 'You've always been brave,' he says, 'impatient, yes, but brave, definitely brave.'

'What do you mean?'

Her dad shrugs. 'Just part of who you are, even when you were tiny, you were never afraid of anything. You must remember that story, the one Mum always tells about when you jumped in the deep end of the pool? You were only two. You saw all the other kids swimming and jumped in, frightened the life out of Elspeth, she had to fish you out.'

Sade has heard her mum tell the story many times. It used to bore her, now she wishes she could hear it again. 'I'm not really that brave, or impatient,' she says at last. 'Besides, what's brave about walking around town?'

'Nothing, I suppose.' He goes back to sipping his tea.

'Well come on then, I've got cabin fever. Let's go out.' Sade stands and puts her tea forcefully down on the carpet, sloshing it slightly. She watches her dad's gaze fall to the dark stain that's beginning to form.

'Sorry, Dad, I'll grab a cloth.'

Searching the kitchen, she is met by a bewildering array of empty grey cupboards and yet more boxes. She gives up and grabs her coat instead.

'No cloth,' she explains to her dad who hasn't moved and still stares at the carpet. 'Let's just go out and worry about it later.'

'You go, if you like Sah. There's too much to do here.'

Sade opens her mouth to argue, but when her dad turns to her he looks so tired that she's grateful she can go out and leave him behind, then feels slightly ashamed for thinking it.

'Okay,' she says in her bright, everything is fine voice, 'I'll be back for six in time to visit Mum.'

She opens the door and steps out into the drizzle, hoping the walk will help clear her head. She crosses the road and stops outside the strange burnt house, checking up and down the street, but there's still nobody about. She must remember to ask her dad later. She walks down Camberley Street towards town, taking deep breaths of the air that tastes stale as well as damp. She wants to feel refreshed but it's as if she's still indoors.

She crosses the road at the bottom, and walks on alone through the empty streets. The only sounds she can hear are her own footsteps and the noise of her steady breathing. She stops, tips her head to one side, bird-like, listening for anything; distant traffic, other people chatting, but there's nothing; only a stagnant silence. She looks up into the dark layered sky. It's heavy, ominous: a solid ceiling of cloud that looms above, threatening. She searches for any glimpse of sunlight, but there's none.

Sade walks on, past the rows of faceless breezeblock houses, each identical to the next. She scans for personal touches, house names, unique hanging baskets, garden gnomes, different coloured painted doors, but everything is the same. The place is more than strange; it's creepy.

She comes to a little precinct of shops, consisting of a launderette, a small supermarket, a hardware store, and a fish and chip shop. She pushes the doors into the supermarket. There are a few people inside

9

milling around with their trolleys, looking blankly at the endless packets and tins. It's brighter inside, but the lighting is still low and the produce looks colourless, as if sitting for a long time in the sun has bleached it.

She chooses a packet of crisps, a banana, takes a milkshake from the fridge and a chocolate bar from the counter at the front. She places the items in front of the shop assistant at the checkout. The woman wears a dark nylon uniform. Her badge reads: *Lindsay, Here to Help.*

'Lindsay,' says Sade making the woman jump slightly, 'that's a nice name. I'm Sade. It's spelt S-A-D-E so people often call me Sadie by mistake, but it's pronounced Sah-Day.'

The woman stares at her blankly, her pale eyes colourless in an unhealthy-looking face.

'We've just moved here, to Stanbridge,' Sade rushes on. She has no idea why she's gibbering so much. 'So, just wondering, you know where stuff is and that kind of thing. I start school on Monday, so I was hoping to meet a few kids first, always helps when you're new to know a few faces, gives you a heads up.'

The woman doesn't say anything, and instead she begins to mechanically sweep Sade's items through the checkout till.

'So anyway, I was hoping you might be able to point me in the right direction, tell me where all the kids hang out? At my old town – in Hexworth – do you know it? It's about an hour and a half north of here, easy drive just up the motorway.' Sade can hear her voice vibrating loudly throughout the shop, but she barely slows to take in a breath. 'So in my old town, all the kids used to hang out in the graveyard, but it's not as creepy as it sounds. You see it was the one place none of the grown-ups used to go, so we were safe to, well to…'

Finally she manages to stop herself before she ends up telling this complete stranger, who looks like she might run on batteries, what she and her friends used to get up to. The shop assistant continues to check her items through the machine, creating a little rhythmic bleep.

The items through and packed in a bag, Sade looks expectantly at the shop assistant waiting to hear some sort of speech, at least how much she owes, but the woman merely points to the display on the till.

Sade pays and turns to leave. Before she does she tries a direct question. 'Is there a graveyard in Stanbridge?'

The woman nods, so Sade at least knows she's understood and the woman can hear her.

'Where is it?'

The woman points to her left. 'That way, behind the church in the town square.'

Her voice is monotone, one single, flat note.

Sade leaves the shop; she pauses for a moment looking back up the street in the direction she came, then turns and walks towards the centre of Stanbridge. I'll show you brave, she thinks.

CHAPTER THREE

Dream Thief

Blythehope is not Stanbridge. There is no Grey, offering him protection. He has no safety net. The decades of devotion to his cause have left Stanbridge a tranquil place of steadiness and calm. The Dream Thief can wander freely around the town, unnoticed by the people who live stress-free lives. It is he alone who has freed them from the torments of their dreams. He has been so successful that he has not had to steal a dream there for many years. People, especially adults, willingly allow The Grey to enfold them. It is as if they are simply rocked into a gentle, all-forgiving sleep.

It would be all too easy just to stay in Stanbridge, revelling in his creation, but he needs his tiny moments of elation. He is called to dreams further afield and must continue with his cause, however dangerous it may become.

Here, in Blythehope, stories of lost dreams have been whispered between the children. The Dream Thief is known, to some, as an evil spirit, talked about as a myth. Even though the children never see him, some watch out for him, trying to scare him off by hanging up dreamcatchers. Silly contraptions of twine, feathers and shells, they hang in the windows like strings of garlic warding off vampires. The dreamcatchers never stop him: weak, pathetic attempts by children who know nothing, who don't know what's good for them.

The Dream Thief keeps low, stops now and then to hide, staying out of sight and keeping safe from all the people that roam freely in Blythehope. People full of colour, stumbling out of pubs, their arms wrapped around one another singing; groups of people barging through the night streets and shouting out like animals; people that sicken him. His face creases into a sneer of disgust at their vulgarity and his clawed nails pull his hood further around his skinny shoulders to shut out the noises of the traffic and the chaos of their crude lives being displayed so openly around him.

In amongst the cacophony of vulgarity he hears other dreams jostling for his attention, but he keeps the original one in mind. Its call is soft and low and he lets it pull him along. He's nearing the house now, away from all the chaos of before. It's a big, detached place, set back from the road, with a gravelled drive, a large front, back and even a side garden.

He shuffles past the swing set, the sandpit, ignores the barking Labrador and scuttles up the side of the building to the window he needs. Without warning, the dream's call stops suddenly. Stealthily the Dream Thief peers through the window to find out why.

The child, from where the dream call came, is a boy, perhaps seven or eight years old. He is sitting up in bed crying. A light is switched on and the Dream Thief shies away, his black eyes sinking further back into his yellowed skin. A man, whom the Dream Thief assumes is the boy's father, comes into the room and cradles his son in his arms.

'Bad dream?' the man asks his son.

His voice is soft and soothing, but despite there being a window between them it is as loud to the Dream Thief's ear as if he's stood beside them.

The boy nods and buries his face deep into his father's shoulder. The Dream Thief curses softly to himself; his voice sounds nothing more than the whine of a persistent mosquito. I'm too late! Yet he stays and listens as the boy pulls back, his face streaked with tears and asks, 'Daddy, where do dreams come from?'

The father gently strokes his son's hair, pulling it back from the boy's forehead.

'They come from your soul,' he answers.

'What's your soul?'

'It's the real you,' says the dad, still petting the boy's head. 'Your soul is the core of who you are as a person. A dream can mean what you want to do, who you want to become, that's why only your soul can make them.'

'But why are they so muddled up then?'

His dad laughs a little. 'Yes they can be weird, can't they? I think it's because your soul and mind work together so dreams can muddle up with thoughts and memories. We sometimes have to unpick dreams or untangle them like a big knot to see what they might mean.'

The Dream Thief waits to see what the boy will think of his father's answer.

'What happens if it gets lost?' asks the boy at last.

'You might forget your dream but you can't lose it.'

The boy's face is thoughtful for a moment. 'Billy Johnson at school told me that your dream can get stolen. Billy said there's this horrible demon who can get inside you and eat it. Billy has got a dreamcatcher. I've seen it hanging up in his window. He says it keeps the demon away.'

'You mustn't believe everything you hear,' his dad answers quickly in a voice that shows that he perhaps doesn't quite like what Billy Johnson has to say, 'especially from your friends. Children think it's fun to scare each another but there's no demon. It's impossible to steal a dream.'

'But what if it does go, what happens? Because Billy says that if the Dream Demon steals and eats it, then you can't ever dream again. He says you become a zombie.'

His dad sighs and lays his son back into bed, tucking the covers around him before he answers.

'Well, we need to make sure we treasure our dreams and keep them safe,' he says at last, his voice still soothing. 'That way our soul can keep guiding us through life and help us to make the right decisions.'

The Dream Thief waits, watching the man try to settle his son.

'Promise me that you'll keep my dreams safe, Daddy.'

'I promise,' says the dad and kisses the boy.

The boy seems reassured by this and snuggles down into his bed. The father turns to leave, switching off the light softly and shutting the door behind him. The Dream Thief sniggers: the noise of a throaty wheeze. Ludicrous advice, he thinks and settles back against the side of the window frame.

He feels no cold, nor does the gentle breeze tug at his cloak as he waits in the shadows for the boy's dream to come again. He is perfectly camouflaged and can wait all night if necessary. Eventually the gentle rhythmic breathing of the boy gives him his cue. He tries to open the window, but it's locked from the inside. He can feel the dream beginning to grow stronger through the glass, the call of it warming up like instruments tuning before a concert. He decides to go through the glass. Less conspicuous than opening the lock and no chill from the outside to awaken the boy. Sometimes he's able to step into the dream through glass, depending on how vivid it is. He imagines himself inside the room next to the boy, and so then, because he's imagined it, that's exactly where he is.

The Dream Thief silently unscrews the lid of the jar as he stands and watches the sleeping boy. He steadies his own breathing, bringing it in sync with the child; in for three, out for two, in, out, that's it, now he can start to see the dream:

> *'Marshmallows are the best for bouncing. Do you think?' I said and giggled.*

'Yes, yes,' said the funny little man with the polka dot hat and shoes made out of jelly. He bounced on four in a row to prove it: a pink one, a white one, a pink and then a white.

'Come along,' he called to me over his shoulder. I was just about to follow him when his face started to change. It melted from being friendly to something twisted and I was too scared to follow. Instead I turned back and saw that the way of the rainbow was open. If I dived into the purple stream I'd float down to the number sevens at the bottom. The landing would be soft.

I tried to leap but my stupid fat trousers caught on something, what was it? Brambles? I turned to pull myself away only it wasn't brambles, it was him.

He'd changed out of his jelly shoes and was wearing a floating black cloak instead. He had me by the ankle. I could see his bony hands. His knuckles looked bruised. The black claw of his thumb hooked round me. My heart was hammering hard in my neck.

I was terrified to look at his face, even though I wanted to, more than anything in the whole world. I could feel his cold grip tightening against my skin. I struggled but he held me firm.

'Boy,' he said. It sounded like a big, angry wasp buzzing inside my head, 'let go, boy, if you try to run it makes it worse. Give your dream to me.'

And I knew then that it was definitely him. I remembered the feathers in my pocket and I pulled them out and threw them at his face. I saw it then,

17

his face, twisted and melted and yellow. A beak nose and eyes so deep inside his head they were almost not there.

I tried to scream, but the noise from me leaked out instead like sick. It came not just from my tummy but also from the whole of me, from the very middle of who I was. I knew that it was my soul that he was stealing and I couldn't do a thing to stop it.

There's the rush, the fast, intense rush of pleasure and now, like sand in water, it starts to disappear. The Dream Thief focuses on the jar in his upturned hand, and the dream slides from him obediently into the glass. He quickly screws on the lid, checks it is tight (he will never make that mistake again) and then turns from the sleeping boy and back through the glass of the window.

He would like to stay to watch the colour seep away, but the dog has begun barking again and it unnerves him. It is best to be away on the long journey home to the house on Camberley Street. Heading back to the safety of The Grey.

CHAPTER FOUR

Sade

She sits in her new school, trying to listen to the teacher's flat monotone. It's something about rules. She needs to learn exactly what's expected of her so that she can blend in with the others, but it's hard to concentrate.

The visit to the graveyard was no use, just a muddy place with crooked headstones, a lonely forgotten church and endless bare fields beyond it. There was no sign of life anywhere. She'd gone back to her dad who didn't seem to realise or remember that she'd gone out. The whole thing was horrible and made Sade miss her mum even more.

The teacher's voice is making her sleepy. Her mind begins to wander. Closing her eyes she thinks of a song about the sunshine being gone that her mum used to sing. She creates an image of her mum walking through the rose garden humming the song. There's the familiar tilt of her mum's head; the embroidered bag filled with useful things swings from her mum's shoulder. Sade watches her mum turn, cup a yellow rose in her hands, lean in towards it and sniff. She watches her expression change to something softer; the little hairs on the edge of her cheek are illuminated in the sunshine. Her mum opens her eyes, turns towards Sade.

'You have to smell this, Sah,' her mum says. 'Come over here; it's like honey. Sade.'

I'm coming, thinks Sade and there's nothing she wants more than to stand beside her mum and smell the delicious perfume, only her body is heavy, reluctant.

'Sade,' her mum says again, the tone of her voice changing.

Sade wants to say that she's coming but the words won't obey her.

'Sade,' her mum says, but her voice is no longer her own and she's pronouncing it differently, she's calling her Sadie, 'Sadie.'

Sade opens her eyes.

'Sadie,' the teacher says again and she's back in the classroom that's painted battle-ship grey to match the desks, the hard-backed chairs, the tiled floors and the uniforms of the pale-faced children. Some of those faces stare at her now, impassive. She's the girl with the bright eyes, the full, rounded body and skin brown from the sun; so different from them.

'Sadie?'

'Yes,' she manages, and more blank faces turn towards her, fish-like, looking but not seeing. They stare through her and beyond.

'Do you understand?' asks the teacher, whose name Sade has already forgotten.

And Sade wants to say that no, she doesn't understand, not what was said to her, not anything and if someone could just explain then perhaps she would be able to do it, be able to cope with all of this nastiness. Only she doesn't, because she's a good girl, so instead she nods her head and says, 'Yes Miss.'

It seems to be the right thing to do as all the children's blank faces turn away from her towards the front once more and the teacher nods and begins to write on the whiteboard. Sade should feel relieved but instead she's beginning to feel as if she's being rubbed out like a pencil mistake.

One face stays looking back at her; the face of the new boy that she knows from somewhere. He's the boy who looks more normal than the other fish-faced kids. He raises his eyebrows at her, a questioning look in his eye. Sade wonders if he sees this place as weird too. She needs to talk to him.

Sade walks towards her new home with the other pupils herding around her, single file, conveyor belt walkers. She remembers the gossiping groups of girls in her old school, the boys kicking a ball or one another. She struggles to make the memory feel real.

'Hey,' says a voice, 'it's Sadie isn't it?'

Sade turns to see the new boy, he half smiles at her, adjusts the bag strap on his shoulder and ambles comfortably beside her.

'Sade, but don't worry everyone calls me Sadie.'

'Oh right, I'm Seb. So it's your first day too? What do you think?'

'Pretty weird,' Sade confesses. 'The whole place gives me the creeps,' she adds shuddering slightly.

'Yeah, I know it's totally freaky right?'

Sade almost stops walking she's so relieved. She turns to look at Seb and wonders what it is about him that's familiar. Could it be his hair, or is it the way he shrugs his shoulders? She can't quite put her finger on it but she knows she has seen him before somewhere.

'What is with the people's voices here?' she asks him. 'They all talk the same way.'

'I know, like one note played over that doesn't go up or down,' says Seb, nodding his head, 'and where's all the colour and stuff? It's like we're walking round in one of those old black and white tellies. God, I'm so glad you're here and can see it too. I thought I was going a bit mad in there.'

'Me too,' says Sade, 'but it's not just in the school, look around you, there's no cars, or pigeons, or anything and I went into this supermarket the other night and tried to have a chat with the woman on the check-out and she didn't say a word to me, it was as if she couldn't even see me. I don't like it here.'

'Me neither, but looks like I'm going to have to stick it out, no choice.'

'I'm stuck here too.'

Sade would like to say more, to tell her whole story to the only person she has met in Stanbridge who seems half way to being normal, but she sees her dad leaning against a wall, a distance away, just as she'd asked.

'Listen Seb, I've got to go, but let's stick together? I reckon we can get to the bottom of what's going on here. I'll talk to you properly tomorrow. Look out for me at lunch and we'll think of a plan.'

'All right, Sade. I'll see you tomorrow.'

Sade looks back across the road. Her dad gives a goofy kind of wave. She smiles and waves back. She wants to rush over and tell him he's made a terrible mistake by making them move. She won't, because she remembers when he told her that Stanbridge hospital was the only place that could help her mum. He said they had to make sacrifices, accept changes in order to help.

'Hi, Sah,' he says, stretching out a hand to carry her satchel.

'Hey, Dad,' she says, but shakes her head at his offer.

He shrugs and they set off for the house together.

'How was your first day in the new school then?'

Horrible, freaky, weird, I hated every minute of it.

'Fine. It went fine, Dad. There's another kid started today too, he seems okay. So how's the new job going?'

'Good,' he says and rubs at the whitening stubble on his chin. 'I think it will be great.'

They walk over the paving slabs together in silence and Sade thinks about the lies they tell each other. She listens for a noise to distract them, but hears nothing at all.

'I thought we could get fish and chips for tea, my treat,' says her Dad.

Not again, thinks Sade hating the thought of the greasy salty taste. She misses her mum's cooking. She misses her mum.

'That sounds great,' she says and links her satchel-free arm through her dad's.

They walk up their path, identical to their neighbours and Sade glances over her shoulder at the house across the street. In the whole time they've been here she's still yet to see a light on. Perhaps it's too derelict for anyone to live there.

'Have you seen the neighbours yet?' she asks.

Her dad is fiddling with the key in the lock. 'Yeah, I said a quick hello to number thirty-three this morning and number twenty-nine popped round last night to see if we needed anything. They seem nice enough.' He opens the door and they walk into the hallway that's still stacked with boxes.

'What about the house opposite?' asks Sade giving it a final look over before closing the door. 'Do you know if anyone lives there?'

'No, not yet, but it's still early days. I'm sure we'll get to know everyone in time.'

'Yeah, we will,' says Sade following her dad into the kitchen, but she knows it's another lie. How can you get to know people who barely talk at all?

Her dad rattles in cupboards, most are still bare, only the essentials have been unpacked. Sade fills the kettle, clicks it on. She leans back against the worktop and looks at the plain walls and matching tiles.

'We could paint the place?' she suggests. 'Brighten it up a little?'

'Hmm?' says her dad, his voice echoing against the cupboard walls.

'The grey,' she explains, 'cover up some of this endless grey.' She sweeps an arm around the room.

'Is it endless?' Her father stands, two teabags gripped in his hand and looks around him as if for the first time.

'Have you not noticed? Everything here is grey.' She stops herself from adding how suffocating it is.

'I suppose it is a bit. Good colour though, grey,' says her dad putting the tea bags in mugs. 'Doesn't show up the dirt and goes with everything.'

The kettle clicks off at that moment as if putting a full stop at the end of his sentence.

'Well, there's too much,' Sade says. 'It's not meant to just go with another shade of grey; there are tons of other colours. How about something bright to break it up? We could paint some crimson or violet or even one of those bright pinks like fuchsia?'

At each colour her father flinches slightly as if the mere mention of them is too dazzling for him to cope with.

'Or yellow?' persists Sade, ignoring his reaction. 'Yellow would be perfect.' She's thinking again about her mum and the roses.

'I don't know, Sade. It looks fine to me, practical and it's been freshly done. It seems wasteful to paint over it.'

'But yellow is Mum's favourite,' says Sade, letting a slight child-like whine creep into her tone.

Her dad reaches out and pulls Sade to him. He's solid enough if a little bony, but he smells different, there's a sort of blandness that's masking his usual smell.

'Tell you what, Sah,' he says and she hears his voice rumble though his chest, 'you can choose whatever colour you like for your own room and they'll be no arguments from me. How's that?'

Sade knows that he's trying to be kind so she nods and mumbles a thank you, but she wants to scratch at his eyes and force him to see this freaky town for what it is. Why can't he see that she, his only child, is having the air forced out of her? Why won't he tell her that Elspeth will get better and the three of them will go back to Hexworth? She wants to go back to their old life, the one with colours and smiles and noises. She wants him to smell right and her mum to wake up and be okay.

As she lays her head against her dad's chest she wills him to say that it will be all right and for her to believe him. She knows, even before her thoughts form properly in her head, that if she wants things to change she can't rely on anyone else. She'll have to do it. She'll have to make it happen. She thinks of Seb and their plan and she smiles secretly to herself. Perhaps she won't have to be all alone after all.

The car wipers go every three seconds. She counts them whilst her dad drives the embarrassingly short distance to the hospital. They should walk, but the drizzle is like walking through clouds so they seek refuge in their tin box. They park and walk quickly towards the hospital and through the doors that open with a swish. It's a strange hospital, made out of countless breezeblocks that remain in many places without plaster or paint, like exposed bones. Pipework runs haphazardly throughout, reminding her of veins and arteries. Only the floor is smooth, polished to a high shine, reflecting back the visitors' worried faces.

They've been here so many times they know the routine, no need to visit the reception that curls round, almost filling the lobby. They head over to the chrome doors and go up in the lift. Sade watches the buttons illuminate, her eyes drawn as always to the red forbidden one for the basement that says: RESTRICTED ACCESS. They climb floor after floor, father and daughter standing quietly side-by-side, until they reach the ninth floor, where they step out and make their way in silence to Elspeth's ward.

A doctor calmly walks past them. Sade wonders how he can be so relaxed when her mum is still asleep. She looks away.

I shouldn't get upset, she thinks.

She dutifully treads the polished blue tiles behind her dad into her mum's ward.

Elspeth is lying back against the stark white pillows. Tubes surround and inhabit her, feeding her everything she needs to stay alive. A machine breathes for her, as she sleeps on, away from life, distant from her family and absent from the daughter who needs her.

'Hello Elspeth,' says Sade's dad and awkwardly picks up the hand free of needles and wires, kissing it. He pulls up the high-backed, wipe-clean hospital chair that sits to attention next to Elspeth's bed and perches on the edge.

'Sade is here too, love,' he adds.

'Hi Mum,' says Sade and gives a pointless wave from where she hovers at the end of the bed.

She hates these daily visits. When her mum had first slipped into the coma, the doctor had told them that talking and touching Elspeth would help. That was the nice doctor from the regular hospital before. Sade liked her. She had a kind way of explaining things. She told Sade that Elspeth was on a kind of journey, that she was trying to find her way back to them, but she had got a bit lost, on the way. She said that if she could hear Sade's voice then she might know which way to turn.

'A bit like if you're on a walk and you lose the person you are with?' Sade had asked.

'That's right, or if you are calling your dog.'

'We don't have a dog,' Sade had said, with a touch of regret.

Sade had believed the doctor, so she had sat with her mum and told her anything and everything. Secrets even, when her dad was not there. She had sung her songs, made up stories, read to her, and sometimes on the days she was frightened, she screamed at her to wake up. None of it had worked. Eventually the kind doctor didn't seem so nice to Sade anymore and when she told her that they were moving Elspeth to a specialist unit, Sade disliked the doctor even more. That's when she realised she would have to fix her mum. These doctors knew nothing. She was the one who knew Elspeth best. After all, had she not been grown inside her? Did they not share the same blood?

Sade knows she can fix her; she just has to find out how.

Sade watches her dad straining close to her mum's face, whispering. He looks tired and older than he should. It's such a sad thing to see that Sade turns her face. Instead she watches the steady up and down of the bellows that breathe for her mum, and the regular blip of her heartbeat on the screen. This is the only sign that her mum is alive at all. Sade feels too hot all of a sudden so she slips off her school blazer and drapes it over the other chair.

'I need to use the loo,' she lies to her dad. She has to get out.

Her father nods, and carries on with his whispering. Sade walks past the curtained bays of the ward, through the double doors and along the high-ceilinged hallway until she's out of sight. She walks through the next set of double doors and onto the following ward.

'It's you,' says a familiar voice.

Sade turns to see Zach, the one she secretly calls Respite Boy, propped up on pillows in a bed in the nearest bay. Zach has been in and out of the hospital since Sade has been visiting her mum. They put him wherever there's space. Sade has talked to him now and again, but he's a funny one and she's not ever so sure if she likes him or not. She's not really in the mood for Zach, but it's better than thinking about her mum so she walks slowly over.

'Hey Zach, how you doing?' she asks in a friendly way.

'Still dying it seems,' he says with that sarcastic

tone he has and as if to prove his point Zach lapses into a horrible phlegm-filled coughing fit that ends in a few disgusting spits into a hankie.

Whilst he's coughing, against her better judgement, Sade sits in the chair next to his bed, and looks at his pile of books. There's one that sticks out a bit from the others and she reads the spine *The Dream Eater*. Sade remembers it. It's the same book he had last time he was on Elspeth's ward. It has this freaky ghoul creature on the front cover and the story is something about a demon that feeds off children. It's a creepy book just perfect for Respite Boy, thinks Sade, nastily.

'How's your mum?' asks Zach.

'Still sleeping it seems,' she says slyly.

'Bummer.'

'Yeah, bummer.'

There's a pause, which Sade fills by looking at the bay opposite, wondering why the curtains are closed.

'So you met my brother then?' asks Zach suddenly. The question throws Sade a bit.

'Eh?'

'Seb? My twin?' says Zach looking up at her earnestly.

'Oh right, yeah, of course, I mean, yeah, I did. I met him at school.'

Sade looks at Zach and wonders why she didn't realise before. She could see it now, the obvious similarity between the two boys, the arching, questioning eyebrows, the smooth, broad forehead, and the thin, slightly pinched mouth. Only Seb is different: he's healthy.

'I know what you're thinking,' says Zach, 'I got all the looks right?'

'Um…'

'Don't worry,' says Zach, looking down at his lap, 'you can leave if you want. I wouldn't want to be stuck talking to a sick kid.'

'It's alright,' says Sade, 'I mean, at least you can speak to me.'

'Not always, sometimes I have a tube stuck down my throat.'

'I know,' says Sade, 'I've seen it.'

Zach stares down at the angry looking cannula sticking out of the back of his left wrist. 'So, Seb says that school is weird, everyone is like washed out or something.'

'Yeah,' says Sade, grateful that the conversation is moving on, 'it's like a horror film. I hate it there; the whole school freaks me out. You should see the kids, they look really strange and they don't talk or muck about or anything. The town as well, it's not like here,' she throws an arm carelessly around indicating the ward. 'The hospital seems to be protected from whatever it is.' Sade pauses. 'Has he been in then, Seb, to see you?'

Zach nods, making the tube in his nose jiggle. 'Just left. Told me that this girl had started in the same year. Said she had loads of mad yellow curly hair. I thought it had to be you. Made sense, what with your mum being sick.'

'Oh right, yeah,' says Sade fingering a loose blonde curl at her ear. 'I'm glad he's there. All the other kids are part of it. Robots. I don't know if I could deal with it if I was on my own.'

Zach smiles slightly.

'What?'

He shakes his head. 'That's what he said.'

Sade looks away, suddenly a bit embarrassed. She glances about for something to distract her and notices the book sticking out of the pile again. Zach sees her looking.

'You can borrow a book if you like?'

Sade shakes her head. 'No thanks. I read one last time you were in with my mum. It was a pretty horrible story. We're probably into different stuff.' She stands up. 'I'd better go; Dad thinks I'm in the loo.'

'Right, okay. Hey listen, Sade, um, see the thing is…I'm in for at least a week for Mum's respite, so come and visit again if you can. I like to know what's going on in the world of the living.'

'I'll try,' Sade promises, 'although I don't think you can call Stanbridge the land of the living.'

CHAPTER FIVE

Dream Chief

The journey back is always longer, and harder. The dream is light, yet it's the weight of the disappointment that he must carry. Three days he's been gone and for what? For another dream that gave a glimmer of pleasure from stealing, then an empty dull ache that he's carried ever since.

He walks up the familiar street, feeling the reassuring heaviness of The Grey, telling himself that this is why he carries on and eventually everywhere will feel as comfortable as Stanbridge.

Now he is on his own street he doesn't have to hide in the shadows – the whole town is in shadow. Only there's something different today, something is out of place. He stops for a moment, checking, his ears twitching in all directions. He lifts his pointed chin into the air, marshalling his senses. There's nobody around, but he can detect a difference. He checks up the street. Some of the houses have lights on; there's a cat walking on a garden wall, looking lamp-eyed in another direction. He sniffs at the air, which is damp but not sharp enough to be cold. Nothing's different after all, he thinks.

He shrugs off the sensations and walks on to the house, feeling the new dream banging against his leg. He's almost home when he sees the light from the house opposite. It must mean that new people have moved in; outsiders. He casts his mind back to try and remember when the house was last occupied, perhaps two or maybe three years ago. Nobody wants to live here. Houses are off-puttingly cheap and yet here they are, a new family, and perhaps within its folds there lurks a child with dreams.

The Dream Thief resists the urge to bound up the wall and peer into the window. He needs to rest, to restore. He tells himself that he will watch in the morning and he forces himself to turn and slide down the chute to his cellar.

The dreams greet him by dancing, exploding in colour and sparkling within their prisons. He retrieves the new one from the folds of his cloak, unties the string and places it on the top shelf. He watches it for a moment as it settles, steadies itself into a deep green rhythmic throb, then he hangs up his cloak and climbs the stone steps into the house. He's long past labelling the jars.

As he reaches the kitchen, the Dream Thief stops, glances out of the window and across the street. There's a movement, a sign of something happening. He shrinks into the shadows, watching. The front door opens, an ordinary-looking man, already being lured into The Grey, walks down the path. The man stops, looks towards the skies, holding his hands out almost theatrically. The man says something over his shoulder. The Dream Thief looks up the path and sees a girl of about twelve. She is bouncy, like an eager puppy. She's so fair, but it is not just her blonde hair, it is the whole of her. She radiates light and the Dream Thief catches his breath. She practically dances down the path towards the man – her father? He watches her as she follows her father, gets into the car beside him and smoothly disappears from sight.

The Dream Thief abandons his plans to wait until morning and begins to get comfortable near the window. He could just await her return, this golden girl of light who literally bursts out of the fog. She's a child so full of life and colour that she looks completely out of place in The Grey of Stanbridge. What fun it will be to steal her dream! What a thrill it will be to make her like all the others. She emits such brightness and flair and she is not even asleep yet. Imagine the vibrancy of her dreams: the emotion and intensity. A dream filled with adventure and challenge. He cannot wait to steal it and feel the buzz as it lifts him into euphoria. Anticipation fills him; how can he sleep now? He settles himself on his chair and rests his elbows upon the table.

As time passes and nothing happens, he begins to feel weary and the excitement of before fades. Perhaps he won't wait up all night, he thinks, and yawns. He stretches out his thin arms and draws his mouth back wide, making his thin lips almost vanish into his skin. He will watch out for them to return and then let himself sleep a little. If she dreams tonight he will hear it and then take his chance.

All I could see was my friend Jamie's trainers. The bottoms of them were black from the dirt off the track. I wanted to be first. He should be looking at my trainers, I thought. The oak tree was always the best for climbing and if you got high enough you could look out over the town below. I could hear Jamie grunting a bit as he edged his way out along the branch.

'Come on, you chicken,' I shouted and tried to shake the branch a bit to scare him, but it was too solid to move.

'You're the chicken,' he shouted back.

I edged out after him and we sat next to one another dangling our feet off the edge.

'Got anything to eat?' he asked me.

I shook my head, even though I had a chocolate bar. I could feel it squashed in the inside pocket of my jacket, but I didn't want to share it.

He put his arms around himself. 'It's getting cold,' he said. 'What you doing for Christmas holidays?'

'Going skiing,' I said.

'You're lucky,' he said. 'I'm going to get a skateboard this year, Mum's promised. You don't get presents at Christmas do you?'

I shook my head.

'That must be rubbish. Presents are the only good thing about Christmas.'

We didn't say anything then for a bit. I looked out at our school in the distance. It was small enough to squash with my feet. I thought about that and about how all the trees around it had started to look naked again.

CHAPTER SIX

Sade

Sade has found a teacher she likes: her art teacher, Ms Farrant.

I'd like to know her first name, she thinks.

Ms Farrant is the only teacher who wears colour. She's more normal than any of the others at Stanbridge High. She has a necklace of multi-coloured beads. The necklace is tucked into her clothes, as if she's trying to hide it away, but Sade has seen it. Ms Farrant wears colourful bright pink tights too. She shows flashes of them from underneath a floor-length grey skirt when she walks on silent shoes around the classroom.

Sade watches Ms Farrant walk up to Seb who sits a few rows in front of her. She sees the teacher stop to look over his shoulder at his picture, and mutter something softly to him.

Sade hasn't had a chance to talk to Seb yet, but they've exchanged a look or two, so she knows that he's still on board.

Ms Farrant was probably once a tall woman, but has shrunk with age. Her wavy hair is almost completely white. She wears it up in a hasty bun from which it jostles to be free, the pins peeking out here and there in a haphazard way. Sade thinks that if the hair were released it would be wild and full of tight curls, just like her own. Wisps of it have already escaped, softly framing her wrinkled face.

This class is not like art in her old school. Here it's called Technical Drawing. The students use rulers, protractors and compasses. They make accurate scale drawings of buildings, or bridges, cars and helicopters.

Sade has chosen to draw a cottage, a cosy one that she would like to live in one day. She thinks she has seen cottages before, but she can't quite remember. Little things like that seem to be slipping away. It hurts to try and keep all of her memories in.

Ignoring the instructions she draws a thatched roof, adding some smoke coming out of the chimney, lead-framed windows, and a little path of overgrown stepping-stones leading up to the door. She would like it to be a blue door, but she has only an array of proper pencils – the complete HB scale.

She senses Ms Farrant nearing. She feels her lean over her shoulder, a faint odour of boiled sweets. Is there a little gasp? Will she be angry about the cottage? The pause stretches long between them as Sade softly shades in the leaves on her trees and Ms Farrant studies her drawing.

'What's this here?' Ms Farrant asks very softly as if she doesn't want the others to overhear. She points at Sade's picture, but doesn't touch the pencil markings.

'A swing,' answers Sade just as quietly. 'A dream home isn't complete without a swing, or,' she adds, 'an orchard.' Sade touches at the picture where the trees are pregnant with ripened apples, 'or a little stone wall to sit on and swing your legs, or here…a lawn full of daisies. Round the back is a pond; you can't see that, because the cottage hides it. It's there though, with lily pads, and it's full of tiny frogs and brightly-coloured fish that swim about and dart in and out of the reeds. I could sit in the sun and watch those all day.'

Sade goes back to shading the leaves on her trees, knowing Ms Farrant is staring at her. 'I need blue,' Sade adds, 'for the door, or maybe it should be yellow. Do you have any yellow, Ms Farrant?' Sade twists her neck to look up at her teacher.

Ms Farrant just stares at her with a face so contorted it's as if she might cry suddenly. The teacher says nothing, making no attempt to answer the question.

Sade glances over at the drawing of the student next to her: a labelled diagram of a lift shaft. There's a cross section that's been enlarged of the pulley system. It looks as if the lift has been dissected. Sade looks back at her own drawing. She wonders if she might be in trouble and opens her mouth to say something, but Ms Farrant has already crept off cat-like to another student. She finds the brief flash of Ms Farrant's pink tights reassuring.

They need to talk to this teacher; she and Seb. Ms Farrant may know something about Stanbridge. Quietly Sade tears off a strip of paper from the bottom of her drawing. She turns it over and writes:

Seb. Stay behind after class. I think Ms Farrant is different to the others. Let's find out what she knows. Sade.

She folds up the note and tucks it into the palm of her right hand.

Fresh paper is stacked on the teacher's desk at the front and Sade gets up with the pretence of needing a new sheet, dropping the note in the middle of Seb's drawing as she passes. She doesn't look at him; instead she keeps her eyes front and gets a piece of paper. When she turns she can't resist a quick look in Seb's direction: he's unfolding the note. She looks around but all the other children have their heads down and Ms Farrant is busy at the back and hasn't noticed anything. Seb reads it quickly, looks up and gives her a brief nod before scrunching up the note and slipping it into his pocket. She returns to her place and carries on with her drawing, a small smile tugging at the side of her mouth.

As the students file out, they stack their art folders on the teacher's desk. The bell rings to inform everyone that lunch is about to be served. Nobody notices that Sade and Seb stay sitting at their desks. The minute the last student closes the door behind him, Sade gets up out of her seat, walks past Seb tapping him on the arm. Together they move to the front of the classroom where Ms Farrant sits looking through a stack of art folders.

'Oh, you're still here?'

Sade nods. She's not sure where to start; worried that too much might frighten Ms Farrant off.

'I was just wondering about the colours,' she tries, gently.

'Colours?' asks Ms Farrant looking bewildered.

'Yes, you see Seb and I are new here and we're used to drawing and painting with colours. Do you have any colours, Ms Farrant, for the class?'

Ms Farrant glances slightly nervously over her shoulder as if someone might eavesdrop into their conversation. She looks from one to the other as they stand patiently waiting in front of her desk. She gets slowly to her feet as if trying to puzzle something out then walks over to the art cupboard behind her and motions for the children to follow.

Inside there are rows of boxes of pencils, neat lines of spray fixer cans, charcoals and white chalks. The paper, of all different sizes is black, white and grey only. Everything is neatly stacked and clearly labelled. Ms Farrant shuts the door and stares first at Seb, then at Sade.

'Where are you from?' she asks them. Her voice barely more than a whisper.

Sade looks at Seb, but she is the one who speaks first. 'We moved from Hexworth, it's a town…'

'I know it,' interrupts Ms Farrant. 'It's beautiful… why? Why on earth would you move from somewhere like Hexworth, to here?'

Sade wants to hug her, this woman, this little old lady with her comfortable shoes and her hidden pink tights. Finally, a grown-up who has noticed. She looks across at Seb who grins back at her, obviously thinking the same thing.

'My mother,' Sade explains, 'has Addison's disease. She got ill really quickly and went into a coma. She was moved to Stanbridge Hospital.'

'Oh, oh…I see, that explains things,' says Ms Farrant, 'and what about you Seb?'

Seb shrugs. 'We're from Blythehope, but it's the same story as Sade.' He scratches at his chin. 'They say that Stanbridge Hospital is the best. They say they've got the specialists there, but I still don't really get why we all had to move. Besides its horrible here…so dull. Where's the colour gone?'

Ms Farrant sighs. 'So it is grey then?' she asks them. 'It isn't just me? You both see it too?'

'Yeah,' says Seb, 'and it's not just The Grey…'

'There are no smells,' interrupts Sade.

'Or noises.' Seb says. 'Nobody laughs, or jokes about…'

'Or screams, or anything; it's like a…sort of flatness.'

'Yeah,' agrees Seb, 'and it's like I'm forgetting stuff.'

'I think I'm starting to forget things too,' Sade adds. She feels less alone the more Seb talks. 'It feels like I'm slipping into a big hole.'

'I'm in the hole, just barely peeping out,' says Ms Farrant. She looks first at Sade then at Seb, trying to decide whether to go on.

'You asked about colour, didn't you? Let me show you both something.' She pulls her beaded necklace from under her grey smock top. At the very end is a key, a brass one. She takes the necklace off over her head and pulls aside the shelves in front. They are on wheels and move easily. It reveals another door, a hidden one. She uses the key to open it and together they step inside. Sade feels like she's on the cusp of something important. Secret discoveries.

There's a cord light switch hanging down beside Sade's head and Ms Farrant pulls it, making a naked orange bulb hanging high above them spring into life. They are immediately submerged in a rainbow of colours.

This is how a real art cupboard should look, thinks Sade. She gazes about her at the stacks of different colour paints, brushes in pots, overalls, coloured card and paper.

'Why don't you use any of this stuff?' she asks, touching things to make sure they're real. Seb, following her lead begins to do the same.

'I tried,' says Ms Farrant, 'in the beginning, but none of the students seemed to know what to do. They just kept using the pencils, choosing the white paper, picking out the rulers, their drawings becoming more and more precise.' She lets out a sigh. 'They lacked imagination, creativity; everything was just a carbon copy of something else.' A flickering touch at the paint brushes. 'Over the years the syllabus kept changing, becoming so narrow, until there was no art at all, only Technical Drawing and all of this became hidden, like someone's guilty past.'

'But why? I don't get it,' says Sade.

'Nor do I, but I found I have to keep it quiet. If you challenge anyone, or ask questions it just upsets people. They don't like too much colour.'

Sade thinks about her kitchen at home. 'My dad is starting to not like colours anymore. He won't let me paint the house,' she says.

'My mum and dad are acting a bit weird too,' says Seb, still touching the coloured card. 'They don't seem to be laughing like they used to. I thought it was just because of having to move from Blythehope, but maybe something else is happening.' He stops and turns to face the teacher. 'What is going on here Ms Farrant?' he asks. 'Why is it so weird?'

Ms Farrant sighs, drops her hand away from the paint brushes. 'I can only tell you my story,' she says.

'Your story?' questions Seb.

Ms Farrant nods and as she starts to speak she sits down slowly on one of the wheeled stools used to reach the higher shelves. 'I was a girl once, what seems like an age ago and it's hard to remember, but there are things that I have managed to hold on to,' she taps at the side of her head. 'Stanbridge was colourful back then. The square, you know the little one in front of the church? It won best floral display of the county three years in a row. There's a little plaque still there, buried in the mud probably.'

'What happened, Ms Farrant?' asks Sade, trying to picture the church square as anything but an eerie place draped in drizzle and darkness, the gateway to the empty graveyard.

45

Ms Farrant looks up at them. 'Call me Maggie,' she says. 'Nobody has called me Maggie in years.'

Sade and Seb look at one another and grin. It's good when you like a teacher, Sade thinks, and it's even better when you have a friend too. Sade feels stronger. A little team is forming: a small army to fight The Grey.

Maggie smiles, but it's weak and quickly fades.

'The colourless happened slowly, like a creeping tide,' she says. She gazes off at something that could be a hundred miles away. 'I used to want to be an artist you know; when I was a young girl I sketched and painted all the time. I loved it. I was always covered in paint, but then one day I stopped. I woke up one morning, but not properly, not really as me. It was as though a part of me was still back in bed sleeping and dreaming. I stopped painting, drawing, everything.' She looks down at her lap. 'The teacher noticed, asked if everything was okay at home. My mum and dad and sisters noticed, asked if everything was okay at school. I didn't even remember painting and I didn't know what they were talking about.'

'I took all the paints and the easel and everything out of my room and put it in the cellar, because it felt like they belonged to someone else and they were so bright they hurt my eyes.' A gesture and glance round at the brightly coloured paints that surround them. 'I didn't even want to be close to them; I was afraid they would burn me, or something, if I touched them. The minute I couldn't see them anymore, I forgot all about them.

'I think I was the first, but then it started happening to other people, other kids, usually younger than me, like little Josie. She was a dancer, really good, lived three doors down from us. She used to dance all the time and was in all of those classes outside of school. One day she just stopped.' She begins smoothing down her skirt. 'I didn't notice. I couldn't even remember her dancing at all; it was only everyone else saying things. It was much later I remembered. I asked Josie about it. She gave me a look as if I was crazy. "I've never danced," she said, just like that, as if she was sucking a lemon.'

Sade's mind buzzes with questions. She uses the pause in her teacher's memories to jump in. 'How come it was only you that remembered whereas everyone else forgot?'

Maggie turns to look at Sade steadily. 'That's what I can't work out, but it has made me feel alone.'

Maggie looks so sad and Sade gets an overwhelming urge to comfort her, but the moment passes, she stays, and the story goes on.

'It was over a few years that little memories started coming back, thoughts and feelings returned. At the same time everyone around me was becoming distant and the colour was draining out of everything. It was like the back of the curtains fading in the sun, or something that you wash and wash until it is left just tired, worn-out and thin-looking.'

'Why did you stay?' asks Seb. 'Why not just head out of here?'

'I did leave,' Maggie explains. 'Once I was old

47

enough I trained to be an art teacher, in your old town, in Blythehope,' she looks up at him softly. 'But I felt so dull compared to all the other students, to all the brightness around me.' She looks down at her feet. 'Something had been taken from me. I could still paint just about and my drawing was good, but there was no real expression to anything I created.'

'I qualified as a teacher and when I started looking for work I noticed the opening here, at Stanbridge High.' She looks up again, staring past them. 'By that time my parents were quite elderly, my older sisters had gone, so I thought it would make sense to come back, to be here for them.' She pauses. 'I think there was something else that made me do it. You see at first I was like you two.' She looks from one to the other. 'I thought I could change things, stop it from happening.'

Seb and Sade exchange a look.

'We do want to know what's happening and why,' says Seb and Sade once again feels so glad he's there.

'There is no reason why,' Maggie explains shaking her head. 'It's just how it is. If you question it, people don't understand. They don't see it as strange; to them this is normal life, how it should be.'

'But it isn't normal,' says Sade, resisting the urge to stamp her foot in protest. 'A hundred miles away from here in any direction is normal, but right here, in Stanbridge, it's freaky. It's definitely not normal.'

Maggie tries to smile. Again it looks to Sade like a weak, frail thing that's not quite real.

'I'm glad you're both here,' Maggie says. 'It's so refreshing to know I'm not the only one.'

'Are you still like us?' asks Sade, smiling a little at Seb and then turning back to Maggie again. 'Do you still want to change things?'

Maggie sighs, looks around her at the colourful art equipment. 'I don't know…I got so tired. My parents both died and I just kind of drifted along afterwards as if this was my lot. I've been like that for years, just accepting things. But I can feel a change. When I talk to you two, I can see that it could be different.'

'Good,' says Sade, 'because we need to stop this, before it takes my dad and your parents too, Seb. There's always a reason why things happen, so we need to find out the reason, discover what or who is behind all of this and stop it.'

CHAPTER SEVEN

Dream Thief

The Dream Thief barely sleeps and when he does it's brief, like a bird that naps on the wing. His mind is always alert, humming under the surface of his melted skull. When the call comes, it is so strong and close that the Dream Thief is practically knocked out of his thin, hard bed. He pushes off the grimy sheet and sits up. An enlarged, pointed ear twitches on its own accord like a horse's, turning and twisting, focusing into the tune of the dream.

'It must be her, it has to be the girl's dream,' he says to himself, words that tangle together incoherently, like a buzzing fly.

He's up, out of bed and down the stairs, barely touching the steps with his bare, gnarled feet and then into the kitchen and up to the window. It isn't her dream that has awoken him. The sound, a low, persistent hum that cascades up and down maybe over three of four low notes, comes from elsewhere. The Dream Thief must find it; he has to have this dream. He wonders who could be dreaming in Stanbridge where The Grey has ruled for over two decades. The thought excites and invigorates him so much so that he is practically fizzing with anticipation.

He rushes down the stone steps that twist their way into the cellar and the imprisoned dreams perform for their captor, twisting and bubbling in and over themselves, vying for his attention. He ignores them as always and instead pulls on his cloak and soft leather shoes, straps an empty jar onto his belt and scuttles out of the coal chute.

The Dream Thief stops for a moment on the wet pavement, twisting his ears every which way until he hears and then feels the call pull at him. It beckons him towards the other side of Stanbridge where a child must be having a vivid and bizarre dream.

The call rises up an octave as the Dream Thief hurries past the girl's house and rushes across the empty streets towards it. He can feel the dream increase in intensity and emotion. He wants to catch it before it changes into something more mundane. It is so much more satisfying if he can enter the dream at the tip of something and feel the energy of the child switch to one of fear.

He passes no one as he rushes on and draws nearer to the other side of the town. The dream's call pulls him up one of the little side streets. He climbs, over a high wooden fence and into a square back garden, up onto a shed and at last to a back bedroom window. The Dream Thief peers inside and sees an older boy, maybe twelve or thirteen sleeping in a single bed. Across the room another single bed is neatly made up. The boy's room is waiting for a brother to make it complete. The Dream Thief sees the uniform of Stanbridge High waiting, neatly folded on a chair ready for the morning. He cannot believe his luck: two families moving into Stanbridge whilst he was away in Blythehope, and here a dreaming boy! Ready and waiting for him.

The Dream Thief pushes against the glass in the sash window, which gives way. He eases it up, just open enough for him to glide through into the bedroom. He can hear the gentle snores of the boy's parents sleeping in the next-door room, but otherwise the house is still and quiet. The Dream Thief slows and steadies his breathing, watching the sleeping boy's twitching eyelids until the dream reveals itself and invites him in:

I knew that I had to keep all the kids moving along, but they were more like cattle that wanted to graze on the long grass we were walking through. Part of me didn't blame them, it was almost knee high and I knew it would probably be delicious if I was a cow, but then they weren't cows, they were kids and no matter how hungry they were we had to keep going. The school site was moving. It wasn't safe there anymore and it was my job to get them into the new hall where we could all get back together and decide what to do.

There was a little shop at the side of the road; it sold tambourines and lemonade by the bucket. I wondered if one bucket would be enough. It didn't matter anyway as the shopkeeper scanned us through the till which took us straight into the lift that went sideways. That was lucky, I thought and we all stepped out into this really bright room. Mum was in there, checking for nits and I could see Zach shuffling around with his drip on a trolley. I was more hopeful now that there were three of us that we'd be able to shift things along a bit quicker. Then came the sound.

It started off as an annoying buzz, a bit like a mosquito in your ear, but it got louder. I was convinced it was a big bluebottle. I was annoyed and turned around to squash it. I was going to ask Mum get one of those plastic swatter things that sit in the corner but then I saw him. As much as I tried to pull my eyes away I couldn't, it was like I had melted in with him. I suddenly felt I might be sick everywhere and over everything.

His eyes were so black they were like never-ending pits and he wore the cloak over his head like Death himself. I managed to tear my gaze away and turned to run for it. I was really frightened.

'Run,' I shouted, worried that Zach would be the first to get caught because he was so weak and frail, but it was me that he was after. Even though I had got quite far down the path he grabbed at me, tearing my T-shirt at the shoulder with his black claws. I saw the back of my brother as he ran for his life. Zach turned to look at me as I was dragged to the floor. My brother's face was filled with terror. I was clawed at until he finally smothered me and there was nothing more.

The Dream Thief lets the rush fill him entirely, billowing out his cloak and ruffling his hood. When at last he opens his eyes he sees the open jar in his hand and by watching it – and only it – the dream drains from him and falls inside. The Dream Thief quickly screws down the lid and stands watching the dream push and pull against the walls of the glass. For a moment he's a little stunned by the power of the boy's dream. He tries to remember the last mission dream he stole, but fails to do so. Dreams with purpose have power and the pleasure he gets from stealing them is more euphoric.

He watches the boy sleep peacefully for a moment or two, seeing the colour seep away from his cheeks and his hair fade just very slightly. He looks across to the uniform waiting for him and knows how much happier the boy will be now. How comfortable and secure the boy will feel in amongst all of the other children the same as him. All the confusion about his life will be gone and it will seem so obvious to him what he needs to do.

Rather than leave straight away, as he would normally do, the Dream Thief decides to explore the rest of the boy's house. It would not do to leave the boy in a home where nobody can understand the changes in him and sometimes, just as a courtesy the Dream Thief will either steal more dreams, or just encourage the grown-ups to slip into The Grey a little earlier than they might otherwise do. He opens the door of the boy's room and glides out onto the landing. He sees the door to what he assumes is the boy's parents' room along the hall and makes his way closer. A little touch on the forehead will be all it needs. Call it a gesture of goodwill.

'The headlights of the car behind are dazzling me,' said my dad.

I swivelled round in the back seat held back by the stupid seat belt that my dad forced me to put on. Why didn't he and mum have to wear them? That's what I wanted to know, but he had just given me one of those stern looks over the top of his glasses and hadn't said anything.

I looked past all the stuff that we had to take with us, jackets, salopettes, hats, bags of food and loose ski boots, to see a car snaking around on the icy road behind. My dad was right; the lights were way too bright. The driver was swigging something from a bottle and his mate was shouting and making rude signs at us with his hands.

'It's too much; I need to pull in somewhere and let them past,' Dad said.

'Try to keep calm,' said Mum. 'I'm sure we can pull in safely soon.'

The driver kept on. Flashing his lights, leaning on his horn and pulling really close behind, almost pushing into our car's bumper. I looked back to the road in front and saw a tight bend to the right. I felt Dad slow the car to take the corner.

The barriers to the side of the road were damaged, with torn gaps in the steel. They looked ripped, but the jagged edges were softened by layers of snow. When I looked out front I saw a big, old truck coming up from the other side of the bend. I heard the rev of the engine of the car behind as it pulled out beside us, straight in line to the oncoming truck.

'Oh my God,' shouted my dad.

The car suddenly swerved into us. I was cannoned into the side of our car. I felt the back seat underneath me lurch to the left. Mum screamed and clutched at the dashboard. Dad battled with the steering wheel, his knuckles as white as the snow outside. Our car skidded dramatically to the left, the back end turning out into the road. I saw the car in front swerve back onto the left side, just missing the truck. I heard the heavy horn of the truck just before I felt it slam into the back of our car. We spun to the right, turning on the ice. Dad lost control and his jumbled words of fear joined in with Mum's screams, and then I felt the car being forced off the road, through the barriers and tumbling, toy-like down the side of the mountain.

The noise was terrible, a frightening scream of metal, mixed with a desperate, deep kind of crunching. Anything not fixed down was flung about, crashing against me, Mum, Dad, the windows, the sides of the car, the roof, anywhere, on and on, until crushing metal finally fixed them in place. I saw, heard and felt it all, right up until, what I later found out was a ski boot, was hurled into the side of my head, knocking me unconscious.

CHAPTER EIGHT

Sade

Sade eyes the back of her dad's navy suit as he rummages in the cupboard for the cornflakes.

'They're on the table Dad, I've told you three times,' she says, pushing the box into the middle from where they were partly hidden behind the milk.

'Well, perhaps you were mumbling,' says her Dad, smiling a bit as he emerges from the cupboard, sits at the table and begins filling his bowl, 'or maybe I need telling four times?' He pours on the milk and starts spooning the cereal into his mouth in a slightly mechanical way. 'So, what excitement lies in store for Sade at Stanbridge High today? Have you got art with that teacher again?'

'Mag– err, Ms Farrant, yeah, for Technical Drawing, just after lunch. She's really nice and she remembers Stanbridge before,' says Sade scraping her spoon against the side of her bowl to get at the little bits of crusted sugar.

'Before?

'Yeah, before it went all washed out and weird.'

'You're not still going on about The Grey thing again are you?'

'Oh, come on Dad, you must've noticed how strange this place is.'

Her dad shrugs, 'I'm not here very much am I? I go to work, I see you, I visit Elspeth. Besides…' he pauses and looks sideways at her. 'I've been thinking and… well…perhaps all of this might be about something else?'

He looks at her with those eyes, the ones he uses when he wants to talk seriously and he's worried how she'll react. Sade can't deal very well with the eyes and if he adds the furrow in his forehead, well –.

Sade sighs, sits back against her chair, pushing her bowl away. 'Go on then,' she says, 'out with it Dad, tell me what you think.'

He reaches out a hairy hand and places it on top of hers, which sits on the table top as if waiting for that very move.

'Sometimes when we get sad we see the world differently from other people,' he begins and she knows what might be coming next. 'It can look and feel like a very cold place when things are not going the way you want them to and you can't change it. But you see…someone who is having a good time in life can easily see all the colour and beauty in the world. To them it's a happy place full of smells and life and laughter. Do you see what I'm saying, Sah?'

'You think The Grey is in my own head? That I've imagined it all?'

'I think,' says her dad slowly, gently stroking the

back of her hand, 'that it's real to you because you're so sad about your mum and you miss her so much. That's what I think and I just want to be honest about that.'

Sade wants to scream at him: how can he be so blind?

But then he says, 'it's real to me too, Sah, this place looks tired and dull and lifeless but I know that I miss her just as much as you do, you know? And that's why I can't see anything as fun or nice anymore.'

Sade looks up at her dad and there is the furrow, deep and real and right across his forehead. Right then she knows she can't do it; that she won't even try to do it, because she will never make him see. She and Seb and Maggie will have to work this thing out without her dad. She knows that it isn't fair to try and make him, he's not strong enough and Sade needs him here and with Mum keeping that part of everything going.

'Perhaps you're right, Dad,' she says, because he could be, couldn't he?

Her dad gets up from the table a little slower and more awkwardly than usual and Sade, knowing that he needs a hug, gets up too. They come together kind of clumsily. Embraced in arms that were once much stronger, she wonders just who is hugging who and where his smell has gone.

'We'll be okay you know, kid?' he mutters into her hair. 'Whatever happens, you and me, we'll be okay.'

'I know we will, Dad,' she says, wondering if they both know that it is yet another lie.

Sade looks for Seb everywhere but it isn't until morning assembly that she spots him. The minute she does she knows something is horribly wrong. She sees the back of his head three rows in front of her and when he turns to watch the Headmaster come in she recognises his profile. He's shockingly different. His face, usually a healthy brown is so washed out he looks ill. His hair is peppered with grey. He stares vacantly out of fish-like eyes, eyes that he shares with all the other kids in his row, all the other kids at Stanbridge High, all the other kids except Sade.

She doesn't have the chance to talk to Seb until break when she spots him walking straight-backed across the playground.

'Seb,' she calls out several times. She has to catch up with him and tug at his blazer before he stops. His face is so different that she feels the urge to cry, especially when he has no recollection of her at all.

'Seb? It's me, Sade,' she offers. Hoping that her name alone will break his trance. That he will remember and everything will be like yesterday.

'I'm sorry? Sade, you say?' His voice is flat, distant and definitely not his own.

'Yes, your friend Sade, you must remember me?'

He shakes his head. 'I don't know you. Are we in the same class?'

'Um, well yes, art, I mean Technical Drawing, you remember our teacher? Maggie?'

'You must be referring to Ms Farrant. I know of her but I don't know any Maggie, or any Sade. Now

I must be going, I want to sign up for extra-curricular maths, please excuse me.'

Sade doesn't wait, she turns and runs, heading straight for the art room. She barges past the other children who barely even notice her, past the Headmaster's door which remains closed, past the school office where the secretary continues typing and past the Head of History who is walking the other way down the corridor but says nothing as Sade flies past him. She barges into the art room where Maggie is sitting at her desk marking a batch of homework.

'It's got him,' Sade blurts out breathless and sweaty. 'The Grey has swallowed up Seb.'

Maggie puts down her pen as Sade flumps down into the seat the other side of her teacher's desk.

'How do you know?' Maggie asks softly.

'I've just seen him,' says Sade suddenly fighting back the tears. 'He didn't even remember who I was. I don't know what to do, he was supposed to help, we were all a team and now there is only me and you and you're not even fully here and my dad thinks the whole thing is in my head and maybe I sometimes think that it is…because you could be just saying things and not really remembering properly at all and what he says seems right because I do miss her and if she was home and awake then everything would be different as she is so bright and funny and full of life and if she was okay then maybe I would feel happier and I would be able to see the colours and hear more things and smell things like yellow roses…'

It all comes out in a big soggy rush and ends with

Maggie handing Sade a handful of tissues that she blows into noisily. The two of them sit there for a while and Maggie lets Sade cry. After a time the emotion slowly begins to settle like dust. Sade recovers, sits herself upright. Ready for a change.

'Do you know what I used to do when I was your age and felt sad?' asks Maggie.

Sade shrugs, 'Paint?'

Maggie smiles, not a full beamer, but a real smile nonetheless. It lights up her face so much that Sade can't help but wonder more about this strange and wonderful teacher and the secrets she might hold.

'That's right, Sade,' Maggie says and jumps up, pulling Sade by the hand to her feet. She half drags her to the art cupboard and taking out her secret key opens up the world of colour. 'Take whatever you fancy,' she orders opening her arms wide at all the paints, 'then take the rest of the day off and go home and paint the walls of your room. I want you to be creative and bold, don't leave any grey, not one tiny little scrap and that is an order.'

The outburst is quite exhausting for Maggie who is forced to sit down, but Sade is exhilarated. Laughing, she uses an old dustsheet as a bag, filling it with bottles of paint of all colours and brushes and pots and all the things she will need. She thanks Maggie by kissing her on the cheek then rushes out of the art room and out of the school. She runs along the damp streets, under the steel grey sky and across the empty roads until she is quite out of puff. Half walking, half running up Camberley Street she heads for her house.

She carries the paints upstairs, concealed in the sheet. She opens the door to her bedroom and lays the bundle down on the carpet, carefully untying the corners to reveal the paints inside. They dazzle in colour, as if they admit their own light. They're not bright, she tells herself; they're just colours.

She knows she must cover her walls. The colours will help, and might even stop her from falling further into the hole. She gets started straight away, putting on an overall and taking out the crimson. She dips in a brush and without thinking about it, paints the outline of a flower on the wall above her bed.

She won't worry if she scatters paint; it doesn't matter if any of it blobs onto her quilt or pillow or carpet. The colour needs to be there. She's desperate to coat her room in brightness, a barrier against The Grey. It could stop her from becoming invisible. In this scary town her room will become her sanctuary, her retreat. The room will preserve her memories, her dreams, which she will not allow herself to forget. She will never become like poor Seb.

She chooses a bright blue, fills in the petals of the flower and then adds a fresh green stalk, a few leaves. She takes the green to the corner of the room, paints a vine that creeps up across the walls over the top of the curtains. A shocking pink comes next and adds flowers to the vine. She paints a flamingo near the skirting board, and another facing it, beaks touching. She adds water, lilies, frogs, tadpoles and fish. She paints a bird, bright white, soaring through the sky, and adds another and another until the birds disappear off into the distance. On the other wall she paints a tree; a long brown branch stretches across the length of the wall like a shadow. On it she paints a yawning leopard, a fly buzzing around his ear, his tail stretching down almost touching the long lush grass below. She paints long-stemmed daisies, butterflies swarming, bees and the seeds of a dandelion clock blowing gently away in the breeze. She paints and paints, feeling alive, feeling free, feeling that she's fighting back.

As Sade paints, it turns darker outside and her dad returns from work. Absorbed, she notices neither of these things, but when she's almost finished she suddenly has the sensation of being watched. Sade stops, turns sharply and walks quickly towards her window. Staring out she sees a flash of movement. She opens the window and still with the paintbrush in one hand she leans out, looks down and catches sight of something scurrying into the bushes below.

She calls out at the thing angrily. She waves a fist and shouts out that she's not afraid, but there's nothing that she can properly see there.

'Sade?'

It's her dad. It's perhaps time for tea, or the hospital. Shuddering, she pulls in from her window, turns back to her room, and is instantly comforted by her own colourful creation. She's not sure that she wants to show her dad her room, he may not understand. She glances at the ceiling. She knows what she will paint there, a big yellow sun, to shine down on her at all times. She never will forget the sunshine then.

'Coming,' Sade calls. She slips out of her overalls

but leaves the paints out. She quickly washes off the paint from her hands and arms in the upstairs bathroom. Glancing at her reflection she sees blotches of paint all over her face and even in her hair. She washes her face then skips back to her room to grab her cap that hangs on the back of her door, shoving her hair inside. She turns to leave, turning off the light and pulling the door shut behind her.

'What have you been doing up there, Sade?' asks her dad. He's spooning some horrible-looking sauce onto overcooked soggy pasta laid out in two spaghetti bowls on the table.

'Homework,' says Sade, pouring apple juice from the fridge.

'Homework has been given out already has it?' he asks.

She nods and tries not to notice how his voice is beginning to sound different, like a ripple flattening out in a muddy puddle.

Sade sits down at the table and picks up her fork. She's hungry, having painted right through lunchtime and despite the unappetising look of the food she's surprised to find it's quite tasty.

'Got any cheese?' she asks.

Her dad produces a bowl of grated mature cheddar, which she sprinkles liberally onto her pasta.

She tries not to notice that her dad has started to eat like a robot; plate, fork, mouth in a monotonous rhythm. She looks down at her own plate instead.

'How was school today?' he asks her.

Completely rubbish as The Grey has taken Seb and I

can see how it's getting a good grip on you too and before long I will be the only one left in this horrible town who can see things for what they are – that is if I can stay out of it and not slip into the hole too.

'Yeah okay I guess, you know, just school.'

'So, you didn't get sick or anything?'

'Sick? No. Why?'

'Oh because I just had a call from…' her dad reaches into his jacket pocket and pulls out a little lined pad, like he's a Detective Inspector who's made notes on a case, 'a Mr Dorchester who says you weren't in his double maths lesson this morning, so he went to check on you at lunch time and again after school. Apparently nobody had seen you since morning break, so he thought you must be ill. But you're not ill it seems?'

'No,' Sade tries to raise her gaze from her plate to her dad's face but loses her nerve, 'but there's a good reason I came home.'

'And that reason is?'

Sade has no idea how she can even begin to explain, so she just rushes in. 'A good friend of mine got kind of, well…he was sort of taken away and it made me really upset and I just couldn't face being at school, with all of those kid's fish-faces and the teachers who just stare out but don't see anything and all that grey everywhere, around even on the floor and the ceiling so that it feels like prison walls closing in and…'

'Oh Sade, not this damn grey stuff again, I don't want to hear it. Don't you think it is hard enough without you ducking out of school and making up stories? Can't you see how hard I'm trying here Sade?

I just need a break…Can't you just be a good girl and give me a break?'

Sade's mouth opens to protest but she stops and watches her dad rake a slightly trembling hand through his hair which looks much thinner and greyer than she remembers and she notices how the skin under his eyes bags and hangs loose to match his bowed shoulders and so she shuts her mouth again and says nothing.

'It's hard trying to remember everything that Mum did for you,' he goes on, but his voice has lost the slight edge of anger, 'and the things that she used to say to make it better for you and I know I'm not nearly as good at being a dad as she is at being a mum, but you've got to do your bit too. You've got to try and make it easier for me to be a good dad. Just go to school, Sade, do the stuff you need to without me having to worry about you, because I've got enough to think about and worry about here.'

Sade feels frightened by his words and the sound of his voice and the way he's starting to look. If she loses him to The Grey who will she have left? She doesn't even know how to fight this thing, whatever it is and now it is taking her dad too. She hates The Grey, more than anything.

'I'm sorry, Dad, I didn't think about you. I will be good, I promise,' she says and watches her dad's face relax a little. His clenched cheeks soften and he gets up, pushing his food away. Sade gets up too and they do their awkward, unfamiliar hug. She knows she has no time to stop this thing before her dad becomes like Seb and barely recognises his own daughter.

CHAPTER NINE

Dream Thief

The girl's coming back, even though the morning is barely over. The Dream Thief watches her from his spot in the kitchen as she hurries along the pavement. She moves with speed but smoothly, as if she's gliding. She wears the uniform of Stanbridge High but the brightness from the flushed skin on her face is dazzling. Her blonde hair bounces around her like a golden light, almost as if she wears a halo. She's carrying something. It looks heavy and a bit awkward for her.

He begins to tingle with the anticipation of stealing her dream. The boy's had been such an unexpected thrill last night and this girl brims with purpose. Her dream will be strong and filled with emotion. He can see she has something important that she must do; people that she cares about are relying on her and she will be dreaming of this and more. All of her emotion will fill him. He can take it from her so easily. He trembles with the excitement of what is to come.

He watches her go up her path, unlock the door and disappear from sight. He wants more. He needs to know what she is carrying and what her task is. After a time, he leaves and crosses the road. He scuttles up the side of her house, scaling the wall. He finds an old empty window box fastened to the brick. He is so slight that he can quite happily be housed in the box and sink down out of sight when necessary. He is able to stand in it and see clearly into the girl's room. He can even use the twine that has been nailed over the wall to scuttle away if he needs to.

The Dream Thief watches the girl paint. She is transfixed. He knows why she's painting her room: she wants to stop The Grey. She must be affected by it after all; perhaps she's weaker than he thought. He sees her attempt to fight it as defiance. It is no matter; it will never work. The minute her dream is stolen, all of the colour will simply fade, like a puddle evaporating in the sunshine.

He watches her paint for so long he loses track of time. He's so lost to his own thoughts that he doesn't see the girl turn. He fails to notice her approach the window, until her face is so close that he can see her breath fog the glass up between them. Quickly he sweeps below the ledge but he can still feel her eyes, those bright, penetrating eyes, looking straight towards his own.

The Dream Thief moves across skilfully onto the latticed wire, bending it, but there's no risk of it breaking. As the girl opens the sash window and leans out, he scuttles down the wire, towards the ground, and hides beneath the scanty branches of privet, near the earth. As he moves, she calls out.

'Is there someone there?'

He waits, as does she.

'I know you're there, watching me. What do you want?'

He crouches low, remains motionless and says nothing but his thoughts are on fire. This girl is different; she is brave and stubborn and more than that, she can sense his presence. He wonders if he should run, but does not.

'I'm not afraid of you,' she bellows and the Dream Thief sees her wave a defiant fist in the air, the other hand clutching a paintbrush. Then he hears the dad and for the first time learns the girl's name.

'Sade,' the father calls for her and the girl turns away from the window and disappears from sight.

The troubled Dream Thief follows the girl and her father all the way to Stanbridge Hospital. He watches them go in, but he cannot go inside. Even being this close to the place is uncomfortable for him. There are very few dreams here and none that call out to be stolen. He has left the hospital well alone and so it has stayed free of The Grey. The whole place is tarnished and even if he wanted to save the hospital and its patients, it is way beyond his redemption.

He shouldn't have come here; it's not helpful to his cause and it's making him weak. He can't risk losing his powers. Without them he will wither away until he's just smoke.

The Dream Thief pulls the hood of his cloak over his head and creeps back the way he came, along the flat, dull streets, back to safety. He slides back down the chute to the cellar, where the stolen dreams dance against their glass in greeting. He ignores them, goes straight to the only dream that gets his attention: the first one. Even though the jar is half empty, the many shades of blue of the dream are still bright. They turn in and out upon themselves just as they always do.

He watches the dream for a while and wonders. He wonders how many years it took before he noticed the dream escaping, until he realised his stupid mistake and screwed the lid down firmly.

He puts the jar back on the shelf. His head aches. The incident with the girl has forced him to think and he doesn't like it. He wants it to stay simple. The dream calls, he steals the power for himself. When he sees the colour drain away he feels proud that it is his magic. The dreams are his collection, his power. Only when there is no colour left, no false hope, will he be free. Everyone will be the same: all will be grey and equal and there will be no pain.

This girl, this Sade, troubles him. The Dream Thief has not been seen by anyone for years; yet this girl can sense him watching and she has no fear. That makes her dangerous. He cannot risk getting caught. She cannot find his dreams.

He is yet to hear her dream. Perhaps she doesn't dream. If she doesn't dream how can he stop her? How can he force her to fall into The Grey? These new questions unsettle him. He thought it would be easy, but what if there is nothing to steal?

His thoughts twist and tumble like the jarred

dreams. He paces around his shelves trying to make sense of what he needs to do. Eventually voices on the street interrupt him. He climbs the cellar steps, and takes his place by the kitchen window.

As he eavesdrops into the conversation between Sade and her dad, the answer presents itself. He slaps his head at his own stupidity. It's her father. He merely has to take her dad and then she will be forced to follow. He watches her father walk stoically up the path and chuckles at how weak he's already become. Like all the best solutions, it will be simple.

CHAPTER TEN

Sade

A noise like the whine of a persistent mosquito wakes her. She sits up and switches on her bedside lamp. It's a bit late in the year for mosquitoes, but as she's prone to being bitten she scans the room trying to find it. There's no sign of the insect. She listens carefully, her head tilted and realises that the noise is coming from the landing, outside her bedroom. She gets up to investigate, climbing out of bed and making her way over to her bedroom door. With every moment she is becoming more awake. The leopard on the wall gives her a lazy nod and she smiles to herself and glances up for the reassurance of the sun above her that she stayed up late to finish painting.

The whining has stopped but Sade decides to go and check on her dad. She opens the door to his bedroom very softly so as not to wake him. It's not her dad that she first sees but a tiny black-cloaked figure that appears to hover at the head of her dad's bed. Although she's shocked she's not scared. She feels sure she's looking directly at the creature responsible for The Grey and the thing that has been watching her. She must capture it. Unfortunately the creature is instantly alert to her presence and it turns, looking straight at Sade. Their eyes lock together and she has a sense of recognition.

The creature is horrifying to look at. Its yellow skin distorts as if it's made of melting plastic. It has a cruel nose that hooks over like the beak of a hawk and a menacing pointed chin. Even though it's disgusting, Sade still feels no fear and stands straight and defiant in the doorway of her dad's bedroom door, blocking what she believes to be the ghoul's path to freedom.

The annoying high-pitched noise starts again and she realises that it's coming from the ghoul. His thin lips are moving. He is trying to speak. Although most of it is an incoherent mix of whining and buzzing, she can still make out a couple of words.

'Let,' the creature says, and 'cannot stop,' and 'be afraid.'

'I'm not afraid of you,' Sade answers and her voice sounds loud and strong, resonating against the walls. Then she says, 'and I will stop you. Now step away from my dad and come with me.'

She lets her gaze drop from where she holds the ghoul's eye to look at her dad. She sees the black claws of the creature's hand touching her dad's forehead but in the next moment it's gone. With a trace of smoke the creature flees through the closed window, passing through the glass, yet miraculously it leaves the window completely undamaged.

The creature moves like electricity, so fast that she cannot hope to catch it but she rushes to the window.

She sees the thing, whatever it is, move quickly in a kind of gliding scuttle across the street and disappear down the side of the opposite house. The house blackened by smoke.

She turns back to look at her dad who lies motionless on his back, his hands laid out by his sides and his feet, heels together sticking up straight making a V-shape under the covers. She watches as what little colour her dad had left melts slowly away until he becomes a washed out imprint, a black and white version of the amazing man who used to throw her in the air and laugh until she screamed with delight.

She looks back at the window but doesn't leave her dad's side. She knows her enemy now and she knows exactly where to find it.

Tinny voices filtered through to me. They were muffled and I wondered for a moment if I was submerged underwater. I could hear a steady rhythmic beeping noise and a nasty, deep throbbing pain beat almost in time with it behind my eyes. Tiny electrical pulses that shot painfully down every nerve ending in my body broke the throbbing. I knew, without trying, that I couldn't move. I could hear my own breath rasping in and out of my chest and there was a sharp smell and taste of antiseptic. Even though my eyes were closed, a bright red light penetrated through and I focused on the colour, seeing the veins running behind my eyelids. I knew I would have to open my eyes but instead I switched my attention to the distant rumble of the voices. They became clearer and I heard my name said as a question.

It was a woman's voice, but not my mother's. I didn't want to hear anything more.

CHAPTER ELEVEN

Dream Thief

It is so easy sometimes, just to invite them in, especially the adults. When he touches the forehead of Sade's father there is no resistance, if anything he's pleased to let go. The Dream Thief watches as what is left of the man's despair begins to drift up and out of his slack mouth, swirl once around the air above him and disperse like steam.

He hears the girl before he turns to see her, breathing in and out as loudly as a dragon. He looks straight at her. Her eyes are so bright! She shows no fear at his face so he warns her that she needs to stop, that she should be frightened of him, for he is the Dream Thief, the one with the power. She shouts her defiant words back at him. He is forced to wait for the moment that her gaze drops, releasing him. Then he flees.

As he disappears across the street back to the safety of the house he is worried, but he knows she cannot resist for much longer. If she dreams he will be there within minutes to steal it and if she doesn't then she will soon fall anyway, rocked into The Grey that surrounds her and all will be calm once again. He has proved that he moves much faster than her and can disappear like smoke. She will never be able to capture him, and although she is brave, she is powerless to stop him.

The Dream Thief calms himself by leaning against the cool cellar wall and watching the dreams. When his anxiety stills, he begins meandering between the shelves, dragging a dirty nail against the odd jar, making the dream move more vividly. He sniggers slightly to himself as he watches the captured emotions, thoughts and memories as they churn and mix themselves. He revels in the extent of his powers before moving on to the next captured dream.

His softly bound leather feet tread so lightly over the discarded labels that he barely even displaces the dust. As he moves about he leaves little trace of where he's been. Removing his cloak and slipping out of his shoes, he climbs the stone steps to get a little rest before he prepares himself for the next, and what he hopes will be the final, battle.

CHAPTER TWELVE

Sade

She knows she won't sleep tonight. There's a sudden and desperate longing for her mum. She wants to ask her mum how she can fight this horrible ghoul that steals the colour from the world. She looks at her dad lying motionless and corpse-like in front of her then turns and walks quickly out of his room.

Going downstairs she puts a raincoat over her pyjamas and some wellies onto her bare feet, grabs the keys from the side and a torch. She heads out of the front door and walks the deserted streets, through the drizzle, towards the hospital. She thinks about everything she has seen and heard and how much she wants to be able to tell her mum.

She reaches the grounds of Stanbridge Hospital and immediately realises how ridiculous her plan is. It's the middle of the night; she will never be allowed to see her mum. Amazingly enough however, there's more life and activity in the car park of the hospital than in the whole of Stanbridge town. She has timed her visit perfectly, hitting the end of the shift change.

She manages to slip into the hospital behind

a distracted-looking doctor and duck into the lift without being noticed. She presses the button for the ninth floor and lets out a breath she didn't realise she'd been holding. Moments later she's there, sitting beside her sleeping mother and lifting her mum's pale, lifeless hand into the heat of her own.

'Oh Mum,' she begins in a breathless whisper, 'I have so much to tell you.'

She lets out the whole tangled story, stroking her mum's hand and at times laying her head gently on her mum's chest.

There's no miraculous response from her mum, but with each word Sade untangles the knot a little more. Muddy thoughts become clearer. Once the whole story is told, Sade is lighter. She knows what she must do next because she remembers where she has seen the creature before.

The ghoul is familiar because he's on the front cover of Respite Boy's book. Though she really doesn't want to, she knows it's time to read the story again. It's the only way to find the chinks in the monster's armour: to learn where and when she can attack it. She has to find Zach's book.

She kisses her mum's hand and lays it back down onto the bed, then leans forward and kisses the paper-like skin on her cheek. She hopes that stopping The Grey might help her mum too.

Respite Boy is in the same bed as before. Watching him in his drug-induced sleep she feels a pang of guilt for not keeping her promise to visit him. The book is sitting, like before, in the middle of the pile on Zach's bedside table. She grabs it and walks smartly back towards the lift. As the doors open, she looks at the front cover of the book. The picture is an uncanny likeness of the disgusting ghoul she saw hovering over her dad. She opens the book and begins to read:

In the beginning there was a land that was governed by demons. The people had to make terrible sacrifices in order to survive. It was not only the crops that they grew and the animals that they farmed that were offered to appease the wrath of the demons but sometimes the gold and precious jewels that they mined and the treasures that they created.

The lift comes to a halt, and Sade puts her thumb inside the book to mark her page. She does a quick check to make sure there's nobody about before heading towards the exit. Unfortunately she's unable to leave the hospital and has to stand and wait for someone who has a security card to let her out. Whilst she's waiting she continues with the story:

The worst and most greatly feared of the demons was the Dream Eater: a disgusting black-cloaked ghoul with a cruel face and black heart. The Dream Eater was driven mad with a desperate craving for more than just what the people mined or farmed from the land. He fed on the very beings of the people; the dreams of their children.

The Dream Eater lived in a deep cave on the

outskirts of the land that was blackened from the darkness of his being. Here he would stay, alone and in darkness only leaving his solitude when forced to feed.

'Hello there, it's a bit late to be here. Are you lost?'

Sade looks up from the book to see an elderly woman's face smiling at her.

'Oh yes, well, I was visiting my Mum only I fell asleep and now I can't get out of the building,' says Sade.

'Well I can help you with that. I'm Dr Burnside by the way,' she says and produces a security card from her pocket. The doctor swipes her card, instantly opening the doors.

'Thanks Dr Burnside, that was kind,' says Sade stepping outside.

'It's no trouble,' says the doctor shaking her head. 'Are you okay to get home? Shall I call a taxi for you?'

'Oh no, that's fine. I only live in Camberley Street in town,' explains Sade. She waves her thanks to the doctor. She notices the smile suddenly drop from the doctor's face at the mention of her street. Sade lets the moment pass and leaves Dr Burnside standing outside the hospital doors. It seems to Sade that it's the doctor, not her, who is the one looking a little lost.

Once Sade is out of the car park and making her way home she opens the book, shines her torch on the pages and carries on reading:

When at last his hunger was such that he was no longer able to control it, the Dream Eater would scuttle out of his cave like a crab and make his way to where the people dwelled.

The people lived in great fear for the lives of their children and made efforts to protect them from the Dream Eater by hanging up dreamcatchers made of twine and feathers. They believed if they could catch the powerful sprites that created mischief in dreams the Dream Eater would feed on them instead and leave their children alone.

One night the Dream Eater, driven by a hunger so ferocious he could bear it no longer, scuttled out of his cave and made his way towards the people. He could hear the tantalising call of a child's hopes and dreams that danced within it. It was less than a day's walk away so he pulled his cloak over his head to mask his horrific face and set off towards it.

When he reached the hut where the child lay sleeping he found the mother blocked his path. She was screaming and wailing for the safety of her beloved son. The Dream Eater tried to warn the woman, but after thousands of years of not speaking, his voice had turned into nothing but a growl. The woman recoiled in horror at this snarling, vicious beast that showed its teeth at her.

In blind panic and fear she began to attack the Dream Eater with clenched fists, but found that she was hitting nothing but smoke. Finally the poor woman collapsed against the wall of the hut, clutching at her sides, weeping and wailing, defenceless against the all-powerful demon.

The beast was unable to feel pity, but there was something still buried deep within him and he knew how to take away the mother's pain. The Dream Eater simply reached forward and touched the woman's forehead with a blackened claw. Instantly the woman fell to the floor and was silent. Her dreams rose up out of her body drifting into the Dream Eater's open mouth and with it went all her hopes, her memories, her loves, her fears, her passion and all of her pain.

The woman was left alive but with her soul so broken she was destined to live an existence less than half of what she had been before, for she would never truly feel anything ever again.

The dreams of an adult were not enough to appease the craving of the beast and so he went on into the hut in search of the child. When he entered the room he found the child not sleeping but awake and calmly looking into the black eyes of the gruesome beast.

'Are you not afraid, child?' asked the Dream Eater, 'for I mean to suck out your dreams and leave you forever but a ghost of what you once were.'

The Dream Eater expected the child to whimper and cower as had all the others when he had spoken, so he was surprised when the child was able to understand him and answered him simply as thus:

'No I am not afraid, for my father is dead from hunting wolves and now you have left my mother as I will become so I shall be forever united with her.'

'But your dreams will be gone.'

'You may have eaten my dreams,' said the child,

'but you cannot kill my soul and l will be as I am now, free of all pain and fear. I will not feel disappointment because I will have no hopes and my life will be calm. And when I finally die my soul will heal and live on in another. It is you, oh demon, with your blackened heart that should be afraid.'

Sade reaches her front door, so she holds her place in the book. Once she's upstairs and back in her bed she carries on reading:

'Afraid?' questions the monster, 'but I am the worst demon of all, I am the mighty and powerful Dream Eater, why should I be afraid? There is nothing in this world that can kill me.'

'And that,' said the child simply, 'is the very reason you should be afraid.'

The Dream Eater roared at these words and took the child's dreams in anger. The child was left just as he had said and the beast turned hastily away and left the hut, returning to his cave.

From that night, however, something had changed in the beast. It was as if the dream of the defiant child had poisoned the Dream Eater for he was constantly in turmoil. He was no longer restless from hunger but from thoughts and emotions that churned painfully inside him.

After much time the Dream Eater could stand it no more and travelled from his cave to talk to the people. He was worried that they would be frightened and unable to understand his words, so with great difficulty he had written down his request on a rolled parchment, which he carried in his clawed hand.

The people were terrified to see the Dream Eater and ran from him, abandoning their tools in the fields and fleeing into their huts. The Dream Eater went to the centre of the town and by the rock in the middle laid down his parchment, then turned and went back to his cave.

When the people believed that he was gone, they came back out of their homes and found the parchment that the Dream Eater had left. The words were clumsily written, the handwriting big, looped and scrawled across the page, but they understood them and the Chief of the people read them out in a strong, clear voice.

'I am the Dream Eater, the most feared of all the demons. I thought that I was mighty and great and that my power was a gift, but it took a child, one of your children, to show me that I am weak. I see now how tired I am and I want it to end. I am to fill in my cave with the boulders that surround it, but when the hunger for the dreams gets too strong it will not hold me, so you need to stop me. Build a great wall in front of my cave. It must be thick and strong, then plant a forest of vines and brambles that no man or beast could ever get through.

Without feeding I will wither away and become nothing more than the smoke of which I am made. Only then will your children's souls become strong again. Do this for your children and for me.'

So the people went to the cave and found that

the Dream Eater was true to his word for it was full of huge boulders. They set to work and built the strongest wall of stone that was bigger than any castle fortress. Then they planted a cruel forest of tangles and spines all around the wall.

Many years passed and the forest grew thick and strong and the people got on with their lives. They still appeased the wrath of the other demons with their gifts but they no longer feared the attacks from the Dream Eater.

One evening, the boy who had challenged the Dream Eater, who had now grown into a man, was amongst his flock of sheep, guarding them against wolves. He was lying out on his back staring up at the sky when he felt a burst of pure happiness. He sat up because his heart was beating with a power and strength he had not known possible and then a laugh, big and from his belly, came roaring out of him. The sheep, which had not seen their shepherd behave in such a manner, looked at him warily and bleated a little. One or two of them even took a few steps away. The man's laughter finally eased. He looked around at his sheep, grinning at each of them, wanting to hold them and bury his face in their wool because finally his soul had healed. He knew, at last, the feeling of pure happiness. He knew that this meant that the Dream Eater had found peace at last.

Sade puts the book down thoughtfully on her bedside table. She's still thinking it over when she falls asleep and then later into a deep and powerful dream.

CHAPTER THIRTEEN

Dream Thief

Her dream! The call is quite shrill and pulses with pent up energy and excitement. The Dream Thief is up and out of bed in an instant. The girl is dreaming; he can hear it! His body vibrates with anticipation, creating a wisp of smoke like a tail wind as he streaks down into his cellar, prepares himself for the steal and slides up the chute. He is over the road and up the side of Sade's house all within a matter of moments.

He doesn't waste time watching Sade as she dreams and trying to blank out the brightness of her room, he passes through the glass of her window and rushes across to be as close to her as possible.

She is curled onto her side, her golden curls fanning around her like the softest cushion and her chin tucked neatly under her quilt. He quickly gets into the rhythm of her breath and miraculously her dream opens itself to him like a stage curtain drawing back at the theatre.

'How annoying,' I thought, as I came around the corner and saw that my mum was still sleeping.

'She would miss the show if she carried on like that'. And what a show it was to be with the great lifting of The Grey by the amazing acrobats in stretchy harlequin tights. I was looking forward to seeing the colours take control once again and watch as the nasty thing shrivelled up into the corner of the room and got smaller and smaller until it was nothing more than a dirty smear of grease.

I knew that I had to get the wake up juice that was squeezed from the berries of hope that grew in their thousands on the mountains of the land of the demons but that would mean I would have to protect my soul. I looked around for the feathers to put in my pocket, but only found a piece of string, which would have to do.

I saw him then, the Dream Eater; he was high up in the corner of the room watching me, like an enormous spider. I knew I was supposed to be afraid of him but he looked so ridiculous up there. He was way too big and clumsy to be suspended upside down like that. I laughed. I laughed so good and hard that my belly hurt and I was doubled over with my hands on my knees. He was so surprised that he lost his grip on the walls and fell to the ground, landing heavily on his back with his arms and legs flailing around. I suppose I should've run away or even squashed him with my boot like a horrible bug. But he looked helpless and pathetic as he sprawled around on the ground like a beetle on its back trying to right itself. It made me stop laughing and reach out a hand to help him up.

He didn't take my hand instead he turned his ugly face away then scrambled up and scampered off. Part of me wanted to follow him because he may have known all the secrets of the sleepy kingdom. But I knew that it was high time I found that Respite Boy and gave him the next clue that would lead him to the woman with the flat face who sold the sweets…

The Dream Thief hovers over the charcoal carpet, right next to the sleeping figure of Sade. The empty jar is still upturned in his hand. He is breathing as heavily as a panting dog, reeling from the power and intensity of Sade's dream. He cannot believe that he simply became part of it. There was no shift to fear at his entrance. She laughed at the sight of him. She doubled over and laughed.

It takes a few moments for the Dream Thief to compose himself. He steadies his breathing. His head throbbing, he screws the lid back on the jar and attaches it under his cloak. He is about to turn and make his way out through the glass of Sade's window when he notices a book on the girl's beside table. It is a small, thin paperback, with a white spine but it is the cover that stops him in his tracks because the picture is unmistakeably of him. He snatches the book up and stuffs it guiltily under his cloak. He hurries to the window, checking the girl by glancing back over his shoulder. The child remains untouched and if anything more colourful than before.

He's been unlucky. He will be able to steal her

dream. He simply needs some time. He will go back, read this strange book, and lick his wounds. He can mull over his defeat of this battle and work out how to win the war.

CHAPTER FOURTEEN

Sade

Sade feels groggy and confused when she wakes. She takes a little time to gather her thoughts as she lies back against her pillows. She relives the image of the Dream Eater creature wriggling around on his back and her laughing at him. She thinks about how pathetic he looked. He was helpless, weak and nothing to be afraid of.

She looks around for the book, but it isn't on the table under her lamp where she left it. She looks under her bed and around the floor but can't find it anywhere.

She hears the noises that show her dad is at least still alive after his gruesome visit, the shuffle of feet on the landing, the click of the bathroom door. She gets up and begins to get ready for school.

As Sade eats her cereal she watches her dad out of the corner of her eye for signs of possible soul damage. With Seb it had been so obvious, but although her dad looks a bit older and less bright than usual she can't see that much has changed.

'How you feeling?' she asks at last as he sits down opposite her and starts his mechanical eating.

'Fine thanks, Sade,' he takes a look at her. 'I take it from your uniform that you're planning on going to school today?'

'Of course.'

'Staying all day?'

Sade rolls her eyes. 'Yes, Dad, I'm staying all day.' So no memory loss then, she thinks, with a tiny touch of regret.

'Good, let's hope this nonsense is all over.'

Sade eats and says nothing for a moment or two until it just bursts out of her in a noisy rush, like a cork coming out of a bottle, 'so you honestly don't feel any different? Because last night when you were sleeping you had a disgusting visitor; I came into your room and the Dream Eater was there. He was hovering by your bed with one of his curly black claws on your forehead. He tried to speak but it was this funny buzzing sort of noise, which is what woke me in the first place. It was different to what it said in the book because in that he growls, but the boy can still understand him. Anyway you're supposed to be damaged and your soul all broken because he's come and eaten your dream and...'

Sade stops suddenly when she finally notices that her dad is staring at her blankly. His mouth is hanging slightly open, his spoon waiting instruction: suspended half way between his bowl and his chin.

'What have you been reading, Sade?' he asks simply.

And she lowers her gaze to her cereal bowl,

because maybe it's just as simple as that. She tries to think about it logically. She read Zach's book last time he was on her mum's ward. It was so vivid she remembered it and it was …at least a month before they moved to Stanbridge. Maybe her dad is right, perhaps she's imagining it all. The Grey, the zombie people, the demon: it could all be in her head.

Perhaps I'm going mad, she thinks.

Her dad says nothing more on the subject and goes back to his breakfast. Sade finishes her cereal, kisses him goodbye. She makes her way with her head down, looking at her shoes all the way to school. If she can just accept it then perhaps it will all begin to feel normal to her.

She doesn't want to look at anything because if she lifts her gaze and sees the identical houses, or notices the flatness of the sky, or listens through the soundless air, or tries to catch the scent of wafting breakfasts, then her dad will be wrong and his dreams will be gone.

I clung to the parallel bars at either side of me. My whole body was covered with sweat. I couldn't see my face but I knew that it was strained and determined because that was how I felt.

'That's it,' said the doctor and although I knew she meant to be encouraging I wanted to punch her.

'Try letting your legs take a little more weight; the muscle is so much stronger. I'm sure you can trust them not to buckle now.'

I didn't want to do that because my legs were nothing but wasted useless things that hung limply from me, but I did it anyway because what else was there? She was right and even though they trembled like mad underneath me they held me up.

I let the weight of my upper body slide down more into my legs, taking the pressure off my arms. I found I was able to wobble my way along the bars to the end. I wanted to sit, more than anything, but the doctor made me turn around and walk the whole length back again. All my muscles were screaming out in protest, and there was a mass of purple swirls in my mind, but I walked back shakily in between the sweaty bars.

'That's excellent work, really good progress, well done,' said the doctor and I was too tired to answer or even look at her face that I still wanted to punch.

'We'll have you on crutches before you know it,' she said and I wanted to cry.

CHAPTER FIFTEEN

Dream Thief

The Dream Thief sits reading on the cellar floor. The ignored jarred dreams are dancing in beautiful harmonised energy on the shelves in front of him. He finishes the book and closes it slowly, turning it over and looking again at the picture on the front cover. He runs a black claw over the hood of the Dream Eater and the movement is slow, almost tender. He raises his head and looks across at the stolen dreams. He begins to think about complicated things like souls and memories and dreams and emotions and how it all tangles together in a way that makes it hard to understand. He wants it to be simple but no matter what he does it gets complicated and twisted in a way he can't control. This girl, this Sade, keeps making him stop and think. He doesn't want to question what he is doing, he knows that it is the right thing and yet...

He needs to remember properly the time when it was clear. He needs to feel certain again that the world will become more peaceful once people are free of their dreams. He knows that once the dream is stolen then there's no more pain. He reminds himself of the simple fact that no dreams equals no disappointment. The more dreams he steals the more peaceful the place becomes; because why fight and argue when everything is calm and steady? And the people are so willing! The adults fall into The Grey without him having to do anything at all. He mustn't forget that the children's dreams call to him, they invite him in, and it is the fear in the dream that makes it easy to steal. That is the emotion the Dream Thief steals; he is merely taking away children's fear. What is so wrong with that?

The Dream Thief watches how the dreams dance for him now, and thinks that surely they would fight; they would resist him if what he does were wrong. This is his calling: he is the Dream Thief.

He discards the book angrily and stands up; he can't let this Sade dictate to him with her strong dreams and silly books. He will stop her by stealing her dream. He will eat and rest and when her dream calls again, he will be strong and he will be ready.

CHAPTER SIXTEEN

$\mathcal{S}ade$

Sade travels up in the lift at Stanbridge Hospital. Her dad is standing straight-backed beside her, looking at nothing. He's already asked her about school over the tea he'd made, a strange concoction of peas, rice and tuna fish. Sade lied, saying she'd chatted and played with her new friends and that no, she didn't find the lessons too boring or difficult. The truth was she'd spent the day trying not to look at Seb or any of the other kids there. She didn't have to worry about talking to them because they hardly ever spoke at all and if they did, it was about completely mind-numbingly boring stuff like how to calculate the circumference of a circle. She'd not seen Maggie all day and for some reason she didn't want to seek her out. The lift pings, saving her from more excruciating silence and they walk together towards Elspeth's ward.

'Do you mind if I visit Res– err, I mean Zach?'

'Who's Zach?' asks her dad, still staring straight ahead as he walks beside her.

'He's that boy that's always in and out of hospital.'

'Oh yes, I think I know who you mean, the boy with leukaemia.'

Sade stops, completely stunned. Her dad stops too and turns back round to face her.

'Leukaemia?' she says, aghast. 'I thought he was in hospital for his Mum's respite.'

'Well it will be. He probably needs twenty-four hour care. He comes here for his treatment too though.'

'What exactly is respite, Dad?'

Her dad gives a half smile and leans forward to rub her shoulder. 'Oh Sah. Respite is what you call a break when it is something medical, so Zach comes into hospital to give his mum a break from caring for him.'

'Oh right, yeah, that makes more sense. I thought… oh well, it doesn't matter.'

They carry on walking towards Elspeth's ward.

'Don't you want to go visit him after all?' asks her dad.

'Um, leukaemia is pretty…well it's serious isn't it?'

'Yes Sade, it's serious.'

Sade gulps, her mouth is dry. 'Could he like, die then?'

'Yes, he probably could, but he could also do quite well. Why don't you ask him about it instead of me?'

Sade doesn't really want to talk to Zach now, but she's cornered. So she kisses her dad on the cheek trying to ignore the sharp cheekbones that weren't so obvious before and turns the other way.

Zach is dozing, propped up by pillows. Sade is pleased to see that there are no tubes around him today and that the skin on his face looks a little pinker than normal. He has a cap on his head as usual but Sade notices strong tufts of brown fluff poking out of it around Zach's temples and ears. She doesn't want to wake him as he looks peaceful. She quite likes watching him, almost as if she is meeting him again, properly this time. She can't help but compare him to his twin. Disturbingly, Zach is the one who now looks the healthier of the two.

She walks over to Zach's bedside table and starts looking through his books wondering if she perhaps imagined taking *The Dream Eater* from him in the middle of the night.

'So you're the book thief then?'

Sade jumps guiltily at his voice but when she turns she sees that he's smiling at her.

'I'm joking, Sade, I said you could borrow them anytime. I don't mind.' He pulls himself up onto his elbows and then up a bit more so that he's sitting more upright against the back of his bed. He takes off his cap and scratches at his head. She can see that his hair is curling as it grows. It looks soft, and much nicer than his brother's, which, since being taken by The Grey, is always slicked back with gel.

'I did take a book,' says Sade. 'I came to see Mum and you were asleep and I just thought…'

Zach holds up his hands. 'It's fine, no problem, just bring it back when you're done.'

Sade bites at the side of her cheek. 'That's just it though, see it's well… I think…' she sighs, then she sits down on the edge of Zach's bed, realises what she's doing and jumps up again.

'What's up with you? You're like freaked out,' says Zach staring at her.

'I am, I know, but there's just all this stuff,' she knocks at the side of her head with the base of her hand. She stops suddenly and stares at him, right into his rich brown eyes, noticing that they're just like Seb's were before-

'Have you got leukaemia?' she blurts out.

Zach lets out an exasperated sigh and slaps the bed with both his arms. 'I don't want to talk to you about it,' he says firmly. He pulls his cap back onto his head.

'Oh,' says Sade, slightly taken aback, 'right, I guess I can understand that. I mean I've never really been that nice to you and…'

'That's why I don't want to,' interrupts Zach. 'See, if I tell you all the stuff about my illness you might change how you are with me. Everyone treats me like I'm going to break and it's really annoying, but you're like just a bit off with me. Call me weird but I like that, it makes me feel normal and not really sick at all.'

Sade smiles a bit and sits down in the big chair next to his bed. 'You're going to kick yourself when you know why.'

'Why?'

'See, you always said you were in here to give your mum respite so I thought respite was like this treatment your mum was getting in another ward or somewhere and you were just in here because she couldn't take care of you whilst she was having her treatment. I thought your family was like mine that you'd moved here because of your mum. I knew you were sick, I could tell by looking at you but I didn't think it was anything that bad, just like you were a bit weak or pathetic or whatever. I even called you Respite Boy. I've been really stupid. Sorry.'

Sade looks at Zach who has a big grin on his face. 'You turkey,' he says, and then lets his smile fade and becomes thoughtful, 'but in a way you're right. I was always the weak one out of me and Seb. He was always running around with his friends and on his bike and stuff and I just had to sit and watch. He always tried to let me into his crowd of friends from school, but I could tell they didn't want anything to do with me and, I don't know, I just sort of hated Seb for it. Jealous I guess.'

He goes quiet for a while and Sade wonders if she should say something about Seb and how he's become like all the other robots at school, but Zach, as if reading her mind beats her to it.

'It's been different though over the last couple of days. Seb's been really weird.'

Sade sits up and leans in a bit closer. 'You've noticed it too then?' she whispers.

'Yeah,' says Zach lowering his voice to match Sade's, 'he's been in to visit a couple of times and he's acting really geeky and his eyes look different; it's pretty freaky. Mum and Dad are like it too, but not as bad as Seb.'

'Just like your book,' explains Sade.
'My book?'

'The Dream Eater? The one I took?'

Zach nods. 'Go on.'

'Well, the Dream Eater is real, a real demon. That's what's happening right here in Stanbridge. I've seen him; he ate my dad's dream and the other night he tried to eat mine, or at least he was in it. I think he stole your book from my table. He ate your brother's dreams and all the other kids at the school. That's why they all look and act so strange, their souls are broken; that horrible demon has broken them all.'

Zach doesn't laugh and he doesn't try to tell Sade she's imagining it, he just simply does what she needs. He believes her.

'That's why Seb is acting so freaky,' he says. 'You know some of the kids back at school in Blythehope used to believe the stories about the Dream Eater. Lots of them had that book and one of Seb's mates, Luke, reckoned he knew someone who'd had his dream not eaten but stolen.'

'Stolen?'

'Yeah. This Luke was at a sleepover at his friend's house and he woke up in the night and saw this little monster with a horrible yellow chin floating near his friend's bed. Luke was too scared to say anything so he just lay there, hiding under the covers and watched him. He saw the monster screw a lid onto a jar that was filled with all these coloured lights, then tuck it under his cloak. Then the monster went through the glass in the window, like it was just made of nothing.'

'That's it, that's him. I didn't see any jar, but I watched him float through my dad's window. Oh my

God, you know this means that he's real then, this demon?'

Zach nods, his expression set and serious. Then he has a thought. 'Why isn't the hospital all grey then?'

'I have no idea,' she answers, still in a whisper, 'but I'm telling you Stanbridge is a town of broken souls. Not one person there is normal. He's got my dad, probably your mum and dad and definitely your brother.'

Zach starts throwing back his covers revealing stripy pyjamas. He hauls his legs out of bed and starts rocking himself towards the edge.

'What are you doing?' she says, jumping up.

'You have to show me, Sade, you need to get me out of here and show me.'

It's a little later in the evening and Sade is pushing Zach in a wheelchair towards Stanbridge town centre. He has a green tartan blanket over his knees and uses Sade's clear domed umbrella to keep off the drizzle. Sade has on her dad's rain hat and a clear poncho. They look a bit like a ridiculous old married couple out for a stroll.

They'd managed to get out just by saying that was what they wanted to do. They wouldn't go far or be long, maybe just to the hospital gardens for some fresh air. Sade's dad seemed pleased that she was making such a big effort with Zach and encouraged them to go out.

As they stroll along a comfortable silence builds up between them. It's Zach who finally breaks it by asking a question. 'So what do the doctors say about your mum?'

'Not much,' says Sade, 'I don't think they know. They just make it up.' She pauses. 'I used to think that I could find some way of fixing her, but I don't know, that just seems babyish now after all this stuff with the Dream Eater.'

Zach sighs and it's so deep it fogs up the umbrella. 'If only we had Dr Dean,' he says.

'Who's he?'

'He was this boy genius. You know the sort, one of those really brainy kids that take all their exams when they're like six or whatever?'

Sade laughs. 'What happened to him?'

'Well he was the youngest ever qualified doctor. He had taken all his medical tests and exams by the time he was seventeen. He was about to start on this amazing medical breakthrough that would be able to re-grow cells…only he disappeared.'

'Where?'

'Well, Dr Burnside always clams up about it and she says nobody really knows what happened to him. I don't like to push it but I think he probably died. It's a really sad story. Both his parents were killed in a car crash and he was in a coma for so long he didn't even go to their funeral. He went to live with his uncle somewhere and that was where he studied and became this amazing doctor. He could've helped us you know, if he was still around. He could've helped both your mum and me. Dr Burnside says he was something else that Jeremiah Dean.'

Sade thinks she's heard the name Dr Burnside before but doesn't have much time to think because they are coming to the outskirts of the town. She pushes Zach over the smooth, flat pavements free of any marks or splodges of old gum

'Look at the houses, Zach,' she says, pointing at the square, featureless boxes that line the empty wet streets like soldiers.

'They're all the same,' remarks Zach.

Together they chat about how nobody makes their house their own by giving it a name or putting up a little painted gate or even growing flowers on their windowsills.

'There are no cars, or people,' says Zach, 'and it's so quiet, like freaky quiet.'

'I know,' says Sade, 'try sniffing the air.'

Zach takes big, noisy sniffs of the air. 'I'm getting nothing,' he says.

They've made it to Camberley Street and Sade points to her house. 'That's our house, it looks exactly like all the others on the street.'

'Except that one,' says Zach and he's pointing to the burnt-out shell opposite.

'I think that's where he goes,' says Sade, lowering her voice to a whisper and leaning over the back of the wheelchair so she's close to Zach's ear. 'I don't think he's really alive, but that house is like the demon's cave in the book. I saw him scuttle his way down the side of it after he took my dad's dream.'

'Let's keep going,' says Zach with a shudder, 'it's horrible.'

'Try living opposite it,' says Sade.

She pushes Zach further down Camberley Street and they walk in silence, looking about until they hit the precinct. The supermarket and the other shops are closed but the fish and chip shop is open and a few people are inside.

'Let's go in,' suggests Sade, 'then you can see what the grown-ups here are like.'

They pretend to be looking at the selection of drinks in the fridge whilst they secretly watch and listen to the people instead. The small queue of maybe four or five customers shuffles steadily down where all the pies and pieces of dried-out fish sit under dim lamps. There's no idle talk about this and that, instead the first person in the queue, (a man with a long dark trench coat and an umbrella hooked over his arm) orders from the man behind the counter who doesn't smile. Four cod and chips, wrapped. He hands over the money, waits for his food and ambles out of the shop. There's no friendly tinkle of a bell as he leaves and instead the next person (a woman in dark trousers and a grey denim jacket) orders, and so it goes on.

'I've seen enough,' says Zach.

Sade wheels him out of the shop.

'We could've stripped naked and danced around in there and nobody would've cared,' says Zach.

'I know,' she agrees. She would find this image funny normally, but it's too sad to laugh. 'Come on, I'll take you to the square.'

She pushes Zach down through the streets until

they come to the sad, muddy looking square in the middle of Stanbridge.

'Maggie says this won best floral display, or something, for like…years.' She sniffs. They stare at the wet benches that stand opposite one another and the tiny splatter of rain that collects into the puddle in the middle of the mud.

'Maggie is your teacher isn't she?' says Zach. 'Seb told me about her. He said that she was really cool and that you were all planning on finding out what was making the town so weird. He was excited about stopping it and I felt really jealous.'

Zach pauses. They stay there together looking out at the wet, pathetic scene in front of them. 'I wished for him to get sick, Sade, I did.' He turns and looks up at her with big puppy eyes through the plastic of the umbrella. 'I wanted us to swap places, just for a day or a week or something, just so he could know how hard it is and I could feel healthy and go on adventures like his.' He turns back round to face the square. 'I could've made that Dream Demon come; this could be my fault.'

'Don't be stupid Zach,' snaps Sade, 'and don't get all drippy on me either. I'm the only one left now and I need you to help me stop this thing. We can't go around saying that it's my fault or yours. We just need to work out how to make it all stop.'

They're quiet for a moment and Sade realises she has been gripping the handles of the wheelchair so hard her palms sting. She lets go and examines the damage. She begins to wonder if she was a bit hard on Zach, but he interrupts her thoughts.

'Look at that tree,' he says and his voice has lifted. 'That's amazing.'

She looks up to see the most magnificent oak tree on the horizon. Its branches streak out haphazardly from its trunk like forks of lightening. As she gazes at it, she feels a glimmer of something deep inside. She knows that if something so huge and majestic can survive in Stanbridge then there's hope after all.

I carried the urns through the dimming light past the shopping precinct. I didn't look at anyone or anything; I knew where I was headed. I made it to the town square, the hanging baskets were alive with colour and I caught the beautiful scent of the lilacs as I hurried past. I rounded the back of the church, trying not to think about the double funeral that I couldn't attend and went through the kissing gate out into the fields beyond. I followed the overgrown but familiar footpath up, breathing deeper to force myself forward.

I finally made it to the tree, the big broad oak with its long, low hanging branches that I used to climb with my friend Jamie, back when I was happy. I gently placed the urns down into the soft, thinning grass below the tree, leaning their backs against the strong aged bark of the tree trunk. I looked up at the branches above me in the fading light and knew that this had to be the place, the only place. Uncle Ezra had agreed that this was a good place too, but I wondered if he would ever come here. He didn't openly grieve for the loss of his brother. He was a secretive man.

Carefully I reached for the bigger of the two urns, the ashes of my father, and prised off the lid with my thumbs. I expected a strong smell, but there was only a slightly earthy scent.

I started where I stood, letting the ashes fall close to my feet. I walked slowly backwards around the circumference of the tree trunk, shedding the ashes as I went until I returned to the spot where I had begun and the urn was empty. I replaced the lid and put the urn gently on the grass. I closed my eyes for just a moment before moving on and lifting the second urn. Again I prised off the lid and going in the opposite direction scattered the ashes as I walked backwards around the tree. I was careful to ensure that I made it all the way back to where I started so that both my mother and father encircled the tree entirely. I replaced the lid of the urn and gently left it in the grass next to the first. I reached into my pocket and pulled out my penknife, and squatting down I found a small, flatter piece of bark that was almost hidden within the folds of the trunk. Taking out the blade I carved an X, and then kissed the tree where I'd marked it. Touching the bark with my lips I could feel the lifeblood of the tree pulsing. I hoped that I had nourished and protected the majestic old oak.

CHAPTER SEVENTEEN

Dream Chief

The call is the same as before, a high-pitched insistent noise, almost like an alarm clock, and instantly he springs out of bed and into action. As he scurries up the wall and through the glass of Sade's window, he reminds himself to stay strong once he's inside the dream.

I mustn't lose focus. I have to frighten her.

He must remember that it is only when her emotions shift to fear that he will get control of her dream.

Once he is beside the sleeping girl, he steadies his breathing and his profile casts an eerie shadow across Sade's quilt. He closes his hooded eyes, and synchronises his breathing. He remains motionless, and makes no sound. Nothing happens.

The time passes, but still her dream doesn't reveal itself. Then he realises that the noise of her call has stopped. He opens his eyes and there she is, her eyes open, awake and staring right at him. She has hold of him with that bright blue penetrating stare and he is unable to move. He has to keep calm and wait for her to lower her gaze. Once she breaks contact, even if it is just for a moment, he will be able to escape, but she keeps on staring right at him.

Without blinking, Sade gets up and moves sideways down her bed and reaches over for her dressing gown. Without releasing him from her laser-like gaze, she throws it over him.

The Dream Thief doesn't struggle; there is something calm about being inside the soft material and he accepts the sensations of the belt tightening around him without worry. He feels Sade pick him up and carry him across her room. She bundles him into what he presumes is her wardrobe. He hears the door shutting and a key turning. He feels safe in here; it's dark, dry and warm and he's away from the glare of those powerful headlight eyes.

It goes quiet. He touches the soft material of the bathrobe that surrounds him and has a sudden longing to fall into a deep sleep.

It has been years since I have really slept.

He lets himself begin to slip towards unconsciousness. He wonders for a moment if he might be dying. He would like to die; what a relief it would be just to let go of the struggle. He imagines it would be like this, just calmly accepting the end. He doubts that he would leave a body behind; there would be nothing. Perhaps a tiny wisp of smoke, just like the demon in the book. He wonders how long it would take but he's happy to be in the moment, to hear only his shallow breath as it rattles slowly in and out of his disappearing body.

It is the noise of voices that stop him being

engulfed. He hears Sade and her dad talking outside the door to her bedroom and begins to reluctantly uncurl his body. He stretches himself upright. He's small enough to be able to first sit and then kneel in the wardrobe, only barely touching the clothes that hang above his head. He wriggles an arm free and uses it to feel around the outside of his body. He finds the tie, made of the same soft material, and exploring, his fingers soon touch the knot. He's able to easily untie it and shake himself free of the bathrobe, which he lets fall into a crumpled heap.

The Dream Thief places his hand over the keyhole. His nail is almost long enough to poke through but he could easily dislodge the key, so he concentrates on the key turning, the lock clicking undone. He has done this hundreds of times with all manner of complicated window locks, so it is simple. It takes only a few seconds before he hears the satisfying click and the door pushes open. He steps tentatively out into the brightly painted room.

He walks towards the window, and then remembers the wardrobe. He goes back to close and lock the door, leaving the empty bathrobe inside, and then effortlessly disappears out of the window. It has all taken such little time that he sits and waits, crouching low under Sade's windowsill in the old plant box, for Sade and her dad to come back inside her room.

CHAPTER EIGHTEEN

Sade

Sade leaves her dream behind and wakes to see the tiny but gruesome figure of the Dream Eater next to her bed. She's neither afraid nor surprised. He is suspended just above the floor with his eyes closed and she waits for him to open them. She watches the flicker of emotion change on his face and notices his ears move the hood of his black cape as they twitch in two different directions.

Once his eyes open, she locks on to them. She knows that she has him. She has the control.

This is my chance!

As she moves stealthily sideways along her bed she can truly study this child-sized, not quite human creature. Its skin is not as sickly yellow as she first thought but more translucent. Its eyes are so pure black she sees no pupils within and she searches them for a trace of anything living, but he appears ghost-like and unreal.

She grabs her dressing gown and bundles it over the top of the creature. The demon, or ghoul, or whatever the thing is, puts up no resistance. She ties the belt up tightly around the creature and picks him up. The ghoul weighs next to nothing and she tumbles it inside her wardrobe and locks the door. She leans her back against the door for a moment to catch her breath then runs from her room to wake her dad.

She knows the wardrobe probably won't hold the creature, but she needs her dad to see and to believe her.

At last I have proof!

Her dad is deeply asleep, flat on his back, arms straight by his side. His mouth hangs open to the side and a sort of throaty snore is coming out. She rushes over to him and begins to gently shake at his right shoulder.

'Dad,' she says softly at first and then increasing with urgency and volume. 'Dad, Dad, come on Dad, wake up Dad.'

Finally after a bit of spluttering, her dad begins to wake. He looks at her blankly for a moment and Sade panics, thinking that he's lost his memory.

'It's me, Dad, it's Sah. You need to wake up; I've got to show you something.'

Sade's dad gives a large, theatrical yawn, throwing his arms into the air in a wide stretch and then shakes his head from side to side like a dog.

After what seems like forever, he finally swings himself out of bed. He dutifully follows his daughter out of his room and onto the landing, muttering a string of complaints at being woken up before he's ready.

'Hush Dad,' warns Sade her hand on the door handle to her room, 'we don't want to scare him off.'

'Him?' says her Dad with sleepy outrage, 'Sade you're twelve and it's…' He pushes up the sleeve of his pyjamas to reveal no watch. 'It's the middle of the night, I hope there's not a Him in there.' He jabs his thumb at the door.

Sade rolls her eyes and opens the door. The wardrobe door is still closed so she tiptoes, cartoon-like, towards it. Her dad shuffles behind her, still yawning, with straight back and squared shoulders.

'This had better be good, Sade,' he warns.

She unlocks the door and dramatically flings open the wardrobe to reveal nothing but a crumbled up dressing gown and a wisp of smoke. Sade hurls herself inside and tosses out the empty bathrobe. She frantically begins feeling the back panels of the wardrobe and then the clothes hanging inside.

'He's gone,' she says desperately from the wardrobe where she is in amongst all the clothes, 'but I was only away for about a minute. He's so quick and nothing can hold him.' She comes out of the wardrobe, her face a picture of disappointment and frustration. 'I don't know how I am supposed to catch him when he's just made of smoke.'

'Who? What are you talking about Sade?'

She sighs and looks at her dad all ruffled, sleepy and confused. She wants to hug him, but then again she doesn't; she wants to hug her real dad.

'I'm sorry, Dad,' she says, 'I guess I was dreaming.'

Her dad says nothing, just turns and shuffles back off to bed. Sade doubts he will even remember it in the morning. She sits at the end of her bed and looks at her paintings on the wall. She's glad her dad was too sleepy to notice them. She goes over to her window, opens it up and leans out.

'This is not over,' she shouts into the unforgiving drizzly night. 'You hear me? I'm going to stop you.'

CHAPTER NINETEEN

Dream Thief

The Dream Thief watches Sade unlock and fling open the wardrobe door. Usually this would make him chuckle, but being caught, having the sensation of being held, he feels different, changed somehow.

He watches the dad groggily swaying, with a complete look of disinterest on his face, as Sade explores the wardrobe searching for him. He sees the look on her face as she emerges and there is a pang of something deep inside him, like a lost thought or perhaps even a memory. As the dad shuffles off out of her room and he watches the girl sit on the corner of the bed, the feeling deepens and almost catches in his throat. She's like me, he thinks, she's tired and wants it to end.

When he realises she is coming towards him, the Dream Thief scurries back down the twine and into the bushes below. He watches from the ground as she opens the window and shouts out into the night, but he knows that her heart is not in it. He can feel her despair. She shuts her window and the Dream Thief wanders slowly and thoughtfully back to his cellar of dreams.

He glances at the cover of the stolen book. The picture really is the creature of nightmares. His face, his whole being, is one to be feared and yet he would like the chance to try and tell Sade why it has to be this way. When he looks at her he can feel, just a little, the pain of her disappointment. If she just let her dream be stolen then all of this would go away. She could be just like the others, free of the battle.

Then there is that small voice of doubt that grows inside him. It comes from the way she fights on. She is so determined, so full of her own self-righteousness. She has her own cause, her own mission to complete. It makes him question everything and wonder about what could've been.

Piles of papers were stacked up all around me and everywhere I looked there were books. Medical books with bits of yellow sticky paper marking important pages and hundreds of pencil notes scrawled all over them. I had a headache, but I couldn't remember a time that I didn't have a headache. Dr Jeremiah Dean: it definitely had a ring to it. I wanted to do it soon, so that I would be much younger than when either my mother or father qualified. I knew more than anyone else my age had ever done.

It didn't matter that Uncle Ezra couldn't understand me, or that all the kids at school looked at me the way that they did. All that mattered was that I studied and became the best. I knew that the only way to stop the constant pain was to learn how to heal, my ultimate dream.

CHAPTER TWENTY

Sade

Sade watches Maggie lean over Seb's shoulder and appraise his drawing. It is probably the detailed interior of a helicopter engine, she thinks sadly. Maggie looks up and catches Sade watching. She gives her a grim smile and a tiny shrug of her shoulders, then pads off on silent shoes to the next student. When Sade sees the flash of her teacher's tights, crimson today, she decides to stay after class. She sits and waits until all the robot kids, including Seb, file out of the classroom before walking to the front.

'I've got so much to tell you, Maggie,' Sade says watching as her teacher takes out her special key, pushes aside the shelves and unlocks the secret cupboard. They go inside and close the door behind them.

'Go on then, tell me what you need to, I'm all ears,' says Maggie.

Sade notices that her teacher looks brighter than when she last saw her, even a little younger. There's more pink to her cheeks, her skin looks less wrinkled and even her hair seems to be turning browner.

'So much has happened. I'm not sure where to start.'

'Just begin from when I last saw you,' suggests Maggie.

'Okay. Well I went home with the paints, just as you said, then I painted my whole room. It was brilliant, all of these ideas just came out of me and I painted loads of things. I even did a leopard in a tree. He's probably all off scale but I'm really happy with him. But then I got this feeling that someone was watching me. I went over to the window, but I couldn't see anyone.'

'Sounds a bit creepy.'

'Yeah, well it is, because it's this Dream Demon thing that looks like a sort of ghoul and that night it came and took my dad's dream.'

'What?'

'I know, it sounds unbelievable but Zach has this book…'

'Zach?'

'He's Seb's twin brother at the hospital? Perhaps we never told you about Zach, well anyway, he has this book all about this Dream Eater, which is a demon that eats children's dreams and breaks their souls. Only he isn't just in the book: he's real! I've seen him. He's a hooded ghoul and I think he's living in the burnt-out house across the street from me. Anyway, this thing has tried to steal my dreams too and he did it to Seb and that is why he is all zombiefied like the other kids, but he can't get mine and last night I caught him in my dressing gown and put him in…'

'Stop, stop Sade, I can't follow any of this,' pleads Maggie waving her hands in front of her chest, 'it just sounds like nonsense. I'm sorry, I can't help but think you've been watching too many horror movies. All this about ghouls and demons and zombies. I mean, I know Stanbridge is dreary, but it isn't soulless.'

Sade sighs and sits down heavily on a wheelie stool. She should've known better than to bombard Maggie with all of this. Maggie is barely out of The Grey herself; she probably had her own dream stolen when she was a kid, just like everyone else in this creepy town. It probably even happened to that boy genius, the one Zach was telling her about that Dr-

'Maggie, do you remember a boy when you were in school called Jeremiah Dean?'

Now it's Maggie's turn to sit down. She pulls up the other wheelie stool and sits opposite Sade so close that their knees almost touch.

'Oh yes,' she says and fiddles with her necklace. 'I remember Jeremiah Dean all right. He was quite a bit older than me, but everyone knew who he was.'

'Zach said he was in a coma or something?'

'He was in a horrific car accident with his parents; the car skidded on ice, crashed through a barrier and tumbled off the edge. Jeremiah was the only survivor.'

'Zach had told me a bit about it. How horrible.'

'When he recovered, Jeremiah went to live with his uncle on Camberley Street.'

'That's where I live, do you know what number?'

Maggie shakes her head. 'There was a fire at the house. Nobody knows what caused it…'

'But, it was that house, the one opposite me, the same house the…' Sade stops herself from mentioning the ghoul again.

'The fire was terrible,' continues Maggie, ignoring the outburst, 'and destroyed everything. Neither of them survived the blaze.' She pinches the top of her nose. 'I find it hard to remember the details of what happened straight after the fire; it was only much later that my memories of Jeremiah began to come back. Some of the kids could remember him still, and they told me about the fire. They never found the bodies – that's how bad the blaze was. They think it just destroyed them completely. I could never go up there, to his uncle's house; it just seemed too horrible. I've not walked up Camberley Street for over twenty years.'

'Twenty years?' says Sade, thinking. 'But wouldn't that mean that you are only in your thirties?'

'Yes, I'm thirty-seven. Why?'

'You look older, younger today than the other day, but definitely older than thirty-seven.'

Maggie says nothing but looks down at her smock top with a funny look on her face.

'I'm sorry Maggie, you still look nice,' Sade gushes. Feeling a little uncomfortable she picks at her nail. 'Can you tell me more about Jeremiah Dean?' she asks hoping to move things along. 'Because Zach says he was a doctor?'

Maggie looks up and at Sade, her face screws up as she tries to pull at a thread of her memories. 'Yes, he was, and very young too. He never got to practise though. I don't think everyone agreed with his ideas at

Stanbridge Hospital, but he had big dreams that boy, very big dreams indeed.'

'What kind of dreams?' Sade asks, thinking, dreams big enough to steal and turn him grey?

'He had amazing new ideas about the human body and how to help it to heal itself. I was too little to understand it in any detail, but they said that if he had lived he would've transformed medicine. It was so sad because all his work was at his uncle's house. He hadn't got the proper permission yet to work up at the hospital and the fire destroyed all of it.' She looks at Sade. 'If you're interested in him you should ask up at the hospital. There was a special doctor there who worked with Jeremiah and helped him recover from his coma, but I bet they will all remember him. His uncle worked up there too, but I think he was just an auxiliary so people might not remember him. His nephew though, young Dr Dean, well he was practically a celebrity in his day.'

'Thanks Maggie, I will ask about him.'

The rest of Sade's day creeps painfully along. She tries to avoid looking at the other kids, especially Seb. Their blank, expressionless faces makes her feel sad; there are so many of them and only one of her. At least she still has Zach. This thought keeps her going; through lunchtime break when she pretends to read in the library, through double maths, through her single file walk home in amongst all the conveyor-belt kids and through her almost silent tea with the stranger in her house who claims to be her dad.

For once, visiting hours can't come fast enough and after a quick hello to her mum she rushes off to find Zach. She can't wait to tell him what she has discovered about Jeremiah Dean. She's convinced that the young doctor's dreams were stolen and that he's still living somewhere in The Grey. After all, they never found his body in the fire. She and Zach can find him together. Maybe they can catch the dream demon again and force him to let go of Dr Dean's dreams. If they can do that then Jeremiah Dean will wake up properly and remember. Dr Dean can wake up and help them both. He can cure Zach and Elspeth too.

Sade rushes round to Zach's bed, but there's no Zach. Instead an elderly woman with puffed-up hair, wearing a paper-thin blue hospital gown, and matching electric eye shadow is sitting up where Zach should be.

'Hello dearie,' she coos when Sade stops and gapes at her.

'Um, hello. Where's Zach?'

'Who you after, lovey? I knew it couldn't be me. I thought to myself when I saw all those blonde curls bouncing up and down. Now she's not one of my grand-kiddies, mind you I've got so many that I could've forgotten one, know what I mean?' She giggles.

'I wanted to see the boy that was in this bed before,' explains Sade.

'Oh, I see. Well I don't know nothing about that, but here's a doctor now, why don't you go and ask her?'

Sade turns to see the doctor that let her out of the hospital when she'd snuck in to see her mum. She runs up to her.

'Excuse me, are you Dr Burnside?' she asks, impressing herself by remembering the doctor's name.

'Yes, that's me and I know you, don't I?' She wears the traditional uniform of a doctor, white coat and stethoscope necklace. The look is complete with three different coloured pens poking out of her top pocket.

'We met the other night,' explains Sade. 'You let me out of the building?'

'Oh yes, that's right, I remember, you fell asleep next to your mum, didn't you?'

Sade nods. 'My name is Sade and my friend Zach used to be in that bed over there.' They both turn and the old lady with the blue eye shadow and bouffant hair waves kindly at them.

'Hello doctor,' the woman calls across to them.

'Hello Maude, I'll be with you in just a mo. Let me just look after this young lady here.'

'You take your good time, my love, I'm not going nowhere,' says Maude, who picks up a magazine and starts flicking through it, licking at a finger with a bright red painted nail.

'Has Zach gone home?' asks Sade, resisting the urge to tug at the doctor's white coat like an impatient toddler.

Dr Burnside turns back to her and Sade recognises the smile she's wearing as the one adults use when the news is not good. Sade's excitement bubble bursts.

'I'm afraid Zach is not doing so well,' Dr Burnside says, and she's using the low and soft voice that grown-ups have.

'Oh,' says Sade. She feels a huge knot swell up in her throat and a stinging in her eyes. She tries to look up into the kind, older, sort of flat face of Dr Burnside but it's too hard to do that so she stares at her trainers instead. She needs new ones; her big toe is almost poking out of her right shoe. 'Can I see him?' she asks; her voice small.

'It's relatives only at the moment I'm afraid. His brother is in with him right now.'

'What does "in with him" mean?'

'He's in intensive care, Sade, and we're thinking of moving him to the hospice in the next day or two if there's no response to treatment.'

'But…it can't be, see he's the last one, nothing can happen to Zach, I can't be all on my own. He has to help me find Jeremiah Dean.' Sade blurts out, in between the sobs, and without waiting for Dr Burnside she flies off to find her mum and dad.

'Wait,' the doctor calls, but Sade runs down the corridor and rushes into her mum's ward. Her dad is sitting in the upright chair next to her mum's bed. It dwarfs him. He is holding Elspeth's hand but stares straight out into space, saying nothing. Sade rushes towards them but is pulled up sharply by a strong, vivid memory. She has so few memories left and this one rushes at her demanding her attention.

She was little, perhaps five years old. She was jumping on her parent's bed in between them and on top of all the Sunday newspapers. They were in their old house. Her parents' bedroom had blue swirly wallpaper and a green-flecked carpet. They had an ancient orange cat called Squash. Squash had been happily asleep on the bed before Sade started jumping wildly. Her parents were cross at first.

'Hot drinks,' and 'crumpled sports section.'

But by the end they were all jumping together and giggling like fools.

How can it have come to this?

She throws herself on the end of her mum's hospital bed and sobs like a thunder storm, loud and wet and without shame.

Sade ignores the crisp, unfamiliar touch of her dad's hand stroking her back and cries about everything she's powerless to control. She sobs because of The Grey, the flat, creepiness of Stanbridge and its people. She cries for Seb and her dad and all the other people who have cruelly had their dreams taken by the grotesque Dream Demon. She cries for her friend Zach whom she believes might die from his scary disease. She cries for poor Jeremiah Dean who lost his parents, had his big dreams stolen and then his uncle died in a fire. She sobs for Maggie who lives half in and half out of The Grey. She cries for her mum, who is lost to the world of sleep and cannot get back, but mostly she cries for herself, because there's nobody to help her and she may as well just drown and be taken by The Grey.

No matter how horrible life is and how difficult things seem, crying can only help for so long and after a time Sade finds the tears stop. Her body begins to recover and although she still shudders, her breathing returns to a steadier rhythm. She lifts her face, which she imagines is bright red and puffy, from her mother's wet bedspread. The first face she sees is not her dad's, who's hand she can still feel on her back but Dr Burnside's.

'I can see how hard things are for you, Sade,' begins Dr Burnside and Sade thinks, oh no, not the caring talk. Dr Burnside doesn't carry on though, instead she's looking at Sade with a thoughtful expression on her face.

'Would you mind if I borrow your daughter for a little while?' Dr Burnside suddenly asks Sade's dad. Before she can open her mouth to protest, Sade is being led by her hand towards the lifts.

The crying hasn't subsided enough for Sade to trust her voice to work without squeaking, so she says nothing. They go into the lift and Dr Burnside presses the B button where it says RESTRICTED ACCESS, then swipes her card. Sade begins to feel excited. They head down floor after floor until the doors swing open into the basement of the hospital, the place that Sade has always wanted to explore.

Here the building is even more bizarre and Sade stares about her, the tears gone. The haphazard pipe-work runs in all directions and in all widths and colours. It reminds Sade of the London tube map. Dr Burnside marches smartly off to her right and Sade tries to keep up without sliding on the polished cream floor. They go past several doors until they stop outside a big one, painted red, with a tiny crossed window at the top. Dr Burnside swipes her card and pushes the door, letting Sade in.

The first thing Sade sees is a huge robotic arm that sweeps in and out, filling hundreds of petri dishes that are laid out on flat pallets. It makes no noise except a gentle sweep when it returns to its base to refill. A technician wearing safety goggles and a paper mask is standing next to the arm, monitoring it. He barely glances up from his work as they walk past.

The entire laboratory is sterile white and there are benches that run like long tables in rows all the way through, creating walkways in between. At certain sections on the benches are separate workstations, each one differing slightly to the next. The one they walk past now has a small round sink and two draining boards either side. The next one has two Bunsen flames burning under a clear flask of bubbling clear liquid suspended in a kind of metal vice.

When Sade looks further along she sees another technician at the next station filling a stack of test tubes with a pipette. And so it goes on and on all the way up to the end around the back and all the way down the other side. The two of them walk the whole way without anyone saying a word and only when they're out of the laboratory and heading back to the lift does Dr Burnside talk.

'This entire floor is dedicated to research laboratories,' she says waving an arm down the corridor, 'just like the one we've seen.' She marches smartly on down the corridor and Sade almost trots to keep up. 'You mentioned Jeremiah Dean; I'm guessing you know a bit about him already?'

Sade nods.

'I was very close to Jeremiah Dean and I know that he would've been a fabulous doctor. It is true that he may have revolutionised our medical practices, but you need to know that the work goes on here without him.'

The lift doors open and they step inside. The doctor presses for the ninth floor, swipes her card then turns to face Sade before she speaks.

'The work at this hospital is tireless and filled with hope for the future. Not just in the care of our patients but in the hours of dedicated research that happens right where we've just been in the hospital basements. Do you understand what I am saying to you, Sade?'

Sade shakes her head and Dr Burnside looks directly at her with serious intensity. 'I am saying that if the staff here at the hospital don't stop believing that, you mustn't either.'

Dr Burnside takes hold of Sade's shoulders. 'You must keep on believing, Sade, because without hope, there's no future.'

The doors open, Dr Burnside lets go of Sade and they both step out side by side. 'I'm going to see Maude now. I trust you can find your way back to your dad?'

Sade nods and Dr Burnside smiles at her. 'You've

got a good future ahead of you, Sade. You must believe in yourself and never give up on your dreams.'

The doctor walks off towards the patients that need her and a much more thoughtful and quiet Sade returns to her parents.

CHAPTER TWENTY-ONE

Dream Chief

He needs to get out and away from all the dreams. The dancing colours and the stupid book are stopping him thinking straight. He pulls his cloak on roughly, scuttles up the coal chute and out.

There are no lights on in her house so he assumes she and her dad will be at the hospital again. There must be someone they visit there, probably her mother. Godforsaken place, they won't help her there. She'd be better off letting The Grey take her. He scurries down the streets not bothering to try and keep to the shadows.

He walks on to the little row of shops where he sees one or two people. Acting on a whim he sidles up close to them. There is a woman in uniform who is coming out of the supermarket. He watches her face as she locks the doors and reaches up to pull down the safety shutter. It is passive, and without expression. For the first time he asks himself if she, like the others in Stanbridge, is happy living in The Grey. She is certainly free of worry. She will have no false hopes for the future. Hopes can only lead to crushing disappointment, but is she better off?

The Dream Thief watches someone else: a man in a baseball cap and dark denim jacket, who is going into the fish and chip shop. The man's face is flat, his eyes blank and he walks to a set rhythm. He stops immediately outside the door and raises his arm, bends it, takes hold of the handle and twists. It is as if the man is following a set of specific instructions. The Dream Thief creeps up closer as the man pulls back the door, enters the shop and joins the end of the queue. Nobody speaks to one another inside the chip shop, instead they stand silently waiting to be served. Are they happy – the Dream Thief asks himself as he watches them from behind the steamed glass? He wonders if he cares.

He pads on down towards the centre of Stanbridge this time not looking at his feet but instead at the sights around him. It is different here from other towns, he knows that, but is it better? It is definitely calmer and it feels safer, more steady and secure, but is accepting The Grey the right thing to do?

When he reaches the square outside the church he looks up at the oak tree behind. Without thinking about the reasons why, that is where he heads.

CHAPTER TWENTY-TWO

Sade

She hangs back from her dad on the walk home from the hospital. He marches mechanically on without noticing her absence.

Without him I can think! The tears felt good, but they got me nowhere. Maybe Dr Burnside is right: I mustn't give up hope.

It's so hard to hold onto that. When she looks at the identical houses, and the small concrete garden walls that separate them, she feels overwhelming sadness. It is like being dead inside.

Everyone that believes her is gone. As soon as they begin to notice The Grey it swallows them up, either that or he comes.

She hates the Dream Demon. If he'd never begun taking the dreams then none of this would have happened and the world would be a better place. Jeremiah would be the miracle doctor that he was destined to become. He would've created the medicine that could fix Zach and her mum.

That horrible creature probably started the fire that killed Jeremiah's uncle, right after he stole all of the young doctor's big dreams.

She is almost outside the burnt house now. Fuelled with venom for the loathsome creature, she strides up to the house's blackened walls, determined to explore inside. She's not frightened of that pathetic shrivelled-up thing. She only has to lock eyes with it and it freezes.

Besides, it always runs away.

There's no gate, only a bare path that leads to a blackened, boarded-up front door. The front top windows are sealed with cheap-looking boards that have been hurriedly painted black. The bottom windows are sprayed with that funny frosting stuff that you can only look out of and not into.

Sade remembers that she saw the creature disappearing down the side of the house, so that's where she heads. She nearly stumbles into what she knows from history class as an old coal chute. I was lucky to notice that, she thinks, where is the grate? I could've fallen down it.

She makes her way around to the back of the house where there's a blackened porch without a door. The wooden frame is badly charred. Inside there's a bench, perhaps once used to change shoes, which has almost rotted away.

She looks up the garden that stretches long into the distance. The fences stand solid either side, but the garden itself is a wild mass of weeds. Nettles grow tall in angry huddles; brambles streak across everywhere and an overgrown monkey-puzzle tree dominates the entire back end of the garden.

She looks back through the porch. The house has been built backwards. The hallway area, with a staircase leading off, greets her. The kitchen must be at the front of the house, opposite to her own.

She's fearful of walking up the steps into the porch, scared that she might fall through suddenly. She tests each step carefully before putting her weight on them. They creak dramatically but hold firm. Slowly she makes her way into the mouldy, charred remains of the porch.

There's a door on the inside, hanging by its hinges like an extremely wobbly tooth. The moment she touches it, it breaks free and crashes noisily into the hallway ahead. She winces against the sudden sound and pivots to face the unwelcoming garden. Nothing stirs. She waits a beat then turns back towards the house.

Bravely, she walks past the stairs, taking in her creepy surroundings: burnt off wallpaper, charred remains of framed pictures so scorched it's impossible to see what they were of. There's a horrible damp smell of aged mould that seeps into her, as if penetrating her skin.

She walks on through the door ahead, which leads to an old-fashioned kitchen. Freestanding cupboards and shelving, burnt and scarred, line the room. A table is set up before the window. There's a chair with a tower of cushions on it, as if ready for a small child to climb up for their tea. A cup and saucer is laid on the table.

Sade looks through the window: a perfect view of

the front of her house. This is where he sits to watch for me, this is what he does. The demon does live in the house; he lives alone and watches me. He sits and waits for the chance to steal my dreams.

She opens a few of the cupboard doors. Mostly they're empty apart from the odd bit of crockery and some strange looking tins and packets. There's no kettle, no pots and pans, nothing that she'd expect to see in a kitchen where somebody is living. She wonders what it eats, and how the creature lives from day-to-day. Perhaps he does eat the dreams, like the demon in the book, she thinks.

She wanders out of the kitchen and goes towards the door on her left. There are remnants of old perished yellow tape over the door, the kind the police use at a crime scene. The door is jammed. It takes her shoulder against it to force it open. The room is completely black, nothing but a burnt-out shell. Anything that had once been inside has been reduced to a thick layer of dried out sludge that forms the carpet.

She can see the wire frame of what she assumes was once a sofa. It stands like a skeleton in the middle of the room. She doesn't want to linger and doesn't even step inside.

She walks past the downstairs bathroom and is about to head upstairs when she notices another door.

It opens smoothly. It is used; he uses it.

There's an old-fashioned light switch on her left, the round kind with a prominent lever in the middle, painted a dark brown. She risks it, flips it on, but nothing happens. She wonders if the ghoul lives without power. Perhaps it doesn't even have running water.

Sade peers through the doorway. Stone steps lead down in a spiral. They look dry and swept. She wonders if perhaps the demon lives down in the cellar. Carefully she makes her way down, becoming more illuminated by an unusual light with each step she takes.

At the bottom she is greeted by row upon row of shelves. Each shelf is stacked high with old-fashioned screw top jars. Jars Sade has seen before filled with sweets in village shops. Most are quite short and stout, but some stretch long like spaghetti jars.

These jars are not filled with sweets, or spaghetti, but lights. Beautiful, mesmerising coloured lights that draw her nearer. They dance a tantalising performance, competing with one another for her attention. Each jar is a different colour, yet they do not stay in one shade of gold, or emerald. The lights ride up and down in a magnificent coloured spectrum. They grow stronger, then dim, fold in and out. Some sparkle, others bubble, none are still. They remind her of a lava lamp she once saw. It was in the window of a junk shop on the High Street in Hexworth, a life-time ago. Only these lights are far more dramatic, far more beautiful, almost as if they are living.

As much as the dancing lights spellbind her, she's also afraid of them. They seem too real, too powerful; as if they are of a different world. She's drawn to them, yet wary of getting too close. There are so many stacked both deep and high on the shelves that they overwhelm her. Almost every inch of the cellar is filled with jar after jar.

The floor is a little dusty and there's a coal chute straight ahead. The same one she saw outside, without the grate. She notices a hat stand in the corner, near the chute, empty except for a little black pull-string bag that hangs neatly from one of the ornate hooks. She walks towards it but slowly, as it means getting too close to the jars.

There's something on the floor near the base of the hat stand that she wants to see. She forces herself closer, trying to keep calm in the presence of so much magic that buzzes and dances beside her. It's Zach's book! He did steal it. She should retrieve it.

Heading towards it she looks down at her feet and notices a piece of paper. She stops, stoops down and picks it up. It's an old label, typed, the sticky back long since turned yellow. She has to dust it off a little to read it:

STANLEY CHESTER AGE 6
DIPPITY DO DOG CIRCUS WITH
MATCHING HATS FOR ALL

She's curious about what it means. Then she notices another one, picks it up and reads it:

SARAH JANE JENKINS AGE 12
CHESS CHAMPIONS DECIDE TO
WRESTLE IN JAM

Looking on the floor nearer to the shelves she can see more of the same. She peers at the jars towards the back of the shelves, forcing herself to edge closer to the magical lights. One or two of the jars have the paper stuck onto the glass.

They're labels for the jars, she thinks. Then she knows that these are the stolen dreams of Stanbridge. He's a thief after all, nothing more than a dirty, rotten dream thief.

A scuffling noise above her makes her jump and she looks around for somewhere to hide but all she sees are the beautiful dreams, jar after jar after jar.

Heart thumping, she flees up the cellar steps, suddenly afraid of what the creature might do if he catches her there. She retraces her steps back out of the house, across the street and into her own home.

She flies upstairs to her bedroom and sits on her bed hugging her knees to her chest. She has no idea what to do next.

I was hunched over the desk in my uncle's house, poring over research papers, and clinical trial documents. I was making notes, feverish copious notes in my illegible, black, scrawling handwriting. I heard my uncle's truck pulling up outside, the slam of the door, and his footsteps as he entered the house, but I blocked it out. I needed more time. The thesis, the papers, would not write themselves. Now that my exams were complete I was officially a qualified doctor. It was only a matter of time before I would be able to formally present to the Hospital Board. My experiments in the cellar were going so well. I knew I was onto something brilliant; it was going to change medical history!

The research team at Stanbridge Hospital would have to commission my work. I knew Uncle Ezra and a few others were against my new ideas and the changes they would lead to but mostly I'd received support and encouragement, especially from Dr Burnside. Once I had the backing of the board I would have real patients to work with and my dreams would come true.

CHAPTER TWENTY-THREE

Dream Thief

The Dream Thief cannot remember a time when he'd slept so deeply. When the call of her dream awakes him, he is startled for a moment and confused by his surroundings. He feels the reassuring bark against his back and the dry soil beneath him. He looks up into the canopy that arches over him, protecting him from the drizzle and remembers where he is. His fingers reach behind him and he feels around the bark gently until he finally touches what he seeks: the little cross.

He should be excited by the dream's call, but it is more weariness than anything that draws him to his feet. He has no jar with him so he must return to the cellar to retrieve one first. As he walks away his ears twitch, straining to hear the last murmurs of the tree branches and the gentle whispering of the leaves. Finally there is nothing except the heavy silence of Stanbridge.

He trudges on past the faceless buildings and along the empty streets until he is outside her house. Her dream buzzes, demanding his attention. He crosses the street and down into the cellar. He turns deliberately away from his dreams, their lights and dance too intense, too blinding for his eyes now. He takes one of the last remaining empty jars, trying not to touch the other glass domes that imprison the dreams.

Before he leaves he stops, wondering if there's a way he can be sure he is successful this time. He turns back to the jars, watching them, looking for one in particular and thinking for a moment or two.

The whine of the dream has become slightly higher pitched and the Dream Thief senses a possible shift in emotion. He has no idea what to expect. This girl is questioning what he believes and has experienced. She has made everything different. He cannot explain how or why, but it is with a slight sense of shame that he is pulled in through her window and finds himself once more next to her as she sleeps.

Again she is curled up like a cat, her blonde hair surrounding her and almost covering her face. Her chin is tucked up neatly under her quilt and an arm is curled protectively around and in front of her chest. Her breathing is rapid and the Dream Thief reluctantly at first but then with greater concentration draws his own breath in and out, breathing in line with the sleeping girl.

The dream is fuzzy at first, like it is being seen through water. The Dream Thief stands as an observer, waiting politely to be invited in.

I had been trying to catch that meatball for ages. It was a huge one, like the horrible ones you get from the cafeteria at lunch only it had a single eye. It had grown spindly legs too that wobbled when it ran. I was swimming in the air after it and I knew that he was on it. That Dream Thief, he was up there riding it like a horse, his black cape flapping out behind him. He made me so mad. I had to catch him. I wanted to shake him until he told me where Jeremiah was.

I kept on swimming in breast-stroke through the air, bobbing up and down for breath and then I heard a voice next to me and saw Maude running beside me. Her funny puffy hair was actually made of bees now I could see it up close.

'Catch him Maude,' I shouted at her.

'What's that dearie?'

'Knock him down.'

But she couldn't run any faster than I could swim and besides she kept skidding on all the tomato sauce that dripped off the meatball. I was shattered and whatever I was swimming through felt all sticky. I needed a rest.

I looked to my right side and there was the swing I had drawn in Maggie's class. I swung on it for a while looking ahead into the window of the cottage hoping to see my mum inside. The window started changing into one of the square ones from the streets in Stanbridge and the sky went from a bright blue to a dark grey. Thunder, I thought.

I heard voices inside the house so I got off the swing that disappeared like smoke behind me. I wandered over to the window and there was an older boy, or maybe a young man sitting at a desk. He had dark brown floppy hair and quite a handsome face that was set in a concentrated, serious expression. All around him were hundreds of schoolbooks with those funny little brightly-coloured sticky notes poking out. There were piles of books and stacks of papers everywhere.

An older, thinner man, who was slightly stooped and had a hooked nose, was standing in the doorway. They were talking. I watched and listened as it played out like an old black and white film:

My Uncle Ezra stood framed by the doorway of my bedroom where I studied. I glanced up from my notes to look at him briefly. He was short, and becoming stooped with age, but he was still a tough, wiry man. The little hair left on his head was smoothed back away from his high forehead.

'Why do you just study?' he asked me. 'When are you going to learn that all of this,' he gestured to the piles of books and papers that had long formed the landscape of my room, 'means nothing?'

'I want to do well,' I said surprised by his directness. He had never really bothered me before; we were like strangers in the same house.

'You can't do well, not really. You think learning all of this is doing well? You think if you pass exams you will succeed?'

My uncle had never understood what I was trying to achieve, but I was alarmed at his tone, he seemed so angry. He could be a bit odd, at times, even a little creepy, but I'd never heard him raise his voice before.

'You need to forget it, forget all of this.'

'I will not forget it, Uncle Ezra; it's all that I live for. It's my life, my dream.'

'Dreams are nothing; you can steal them away, just like this.' He clicked his long, strong fingers. The sound was sharp and resonated throughout the room and I began to feel afraid of him.

'It is time for me to take control,' said Uncle Ezra with a serious finality. 'It has gone too far. It stops. I will stop it tonight.'

I watched in disbelief as my uncle began gathering up papers and books. Holding great armfuls he left my bedroom, and headed for the top of the stairs. I jumped up, knocking over the stool behind me.

'Where are you going with those?' I demanded. 'Where are you taking them?'

I followed my uncle downstairs, into the lounge where a fire blazed in the grate. I watched in horror as my uncle began to throw the lot into the flames. There were too many and some spilt out over the hearth, but my uncle made no attempt to control or contain the fire.

'No,' I shouted, 'Uncle Ezra, please stop, you can't do this.'

I grabbed at him. He shook me off his arm and went back up to my bedroom. He took another stack of books. I pleaded and begged as I followed him but he acted with steely determination and fed the roaring fire with yet more and more fuel.

I became desperate, grabbing at the papers he carried, trying to pull them free of his vice-like grip, I screamed at him to stop.

150

'Get out of the way, boy, before I make you.'

I stepped back, shocked at his ferocity. I knew that he, like some of the others at Stanbridge Hospital was against the ideas that I had, but he was my uncle, and I wasn't expecting this. Perhaps he had become mad. He had never been a loving guardian to me, distant and sometimes cold, but never cruel. He was ruining my chances, destroying my dreams.

'This is something that has to stop,' said my uncle. His voice was raised above the noise of the greedy fire that was spreading free of its constraints. 'It can't go on.'

'No, no, please don't burn these things,' I begged, but I was being forced backwards away from my crazed uncle by the intense heat. 'This is how I learn, how I can help to heal people. Without this knowledge nobody will back my work. I can cure people, I know I can.'

'You can't cure people; it's all just stupid dreams.'

My uncle fed more and more into the fire and I thought about my on-going experiments in the cellar. What if Uncle Ezra had found them? I stood back for a moment, unsure what to do. My uncle sensed the change.

'So you're starting to see sense now then, boy? You can see all of this is pointless, a worthless waste of time? Then help me, help me to destroy it, gather everything; let's burn it together. Look how she burns, Jeremiah, doesn't she burn bright, let's make her go higher. Burn it, burn it all.'

My uncle had the look of madness in his eye;

his hair usually so smooth against his head, stuck up haphazard in all ways and he had soot marks up his arms, across his face. He glistened with sweat, as the room heated up like a furnace. I backed further away, afraid of what he was turning into and what he might do next. I glanced from the doorway of the lounge to the cellar door behind me and my uncle caught my look.

'What are you worried about, boy? You're not scared of a little fire are you?' He was almost shouting now above the roar of the blaze. 'Oh, wait, I know what it is, how stupid of me to think you would be on my side.' Uncle Ezra stood up straighter and smacked the palm of his hand against his forehead. 'You're thinking of these, aren't you?'

He reached behind the sofa and pulled out an empty jar, threw it across the room to me and I caught it in my arms. The glass was hot and I could feel it burn the skin on my arms slightly, even through the thick sleeves of my cardigan.

'You're thinking of your jars, not that empty one, but the ones with those creepy bits of body floating around inside their glass domes. What? You think I never found them? I saw those months ago. I kept waiting for you to come to your senses, but it ends tonight. I will end it all.'

My uncle reached behind the sofa, but it was so hot inside the room that I couldn't follow him. I watched in horror as he emerged wet with sweat, a jar raised high in his hands, up in the air above his head. 'They're all here, your gruesome little collection, and I will burn the lot.'

'Uncle, wait,' I screamed, 'don't! It's too much; they're flammable, highly flammable.'

But Uncle Ezra refused to listen. He threw the jar into the fire. There was a moment or two before the heat got through to the sealed container. I used that precious time to try and save my uncle.

'Run, get out of here, Uncle Ezra. The whole house will blow up; we need to get out.'

But that was all I did. I did not wait for my last living relative; instead I turned and ran for the back porch. I made it to the back door before the blast caught me and it was strong enough to throw me out onto the grass. I covered my head and face with my arms as the blast smashed the glass out of the windows. I scrambled to my feet and blind with tears I ran as far and as fast as I could.

I watched the boy running off. The house was ablaze, with plumes of thick, black smoke billowing up like mushroom clouds. I could no longer see Uncle Ezra but I knew that I was watching the making of the Dream Thief. The melted skin, the cruel need to steal children's dreams; he was the uncle that never really died. Uncle Ezra had turned into the Dream Thief that night and he stayed living in his house that became nothing more than a burnt-out shell.

The Dream Thief forces himself out of Sade's dream. He drives his trembling body backwards, breaking the dream's surface like skin on water. He stands dazed and weak for a few moments before collapsing in exhaustion onto the grey-carpeted floor of Sade's bedroom.

CHAPTER TWENTY-FOUR

Sade

'You're Uncle Ezra,' Sade says, 'or at least you were once. The fire and then stealing all those dreams has changed you into something disgusting.'

She's standing on her bed wide awake, pointing down accusingly at the Dream Thief who's merely a heap of black that lies half-dead on the floor at the base of her bed.

'You're not even human anymore. You're horrible and you deserve to just wither away and die for what you've done.'

The vivid dream has awoken Sade and told her everything she needs to know. She waits for Jeremiah's uncle to defend himself, but there is no reply. She notices that the Dream Thief clutches an open jar in his arms, cradling it to him like a baby.

'You brought one of Jeremiah's dreams with you didn't you?' she says. 'You let it out so I could see it, but why? Did you think that it would frighten me into giving you mine?'

The Dream Thief says nothing and lies motionless before her as if defeated.

'Look at you,' spits Sade. 'You're weak, you're pathetic. How could you do that to poor Jeremiah, your own nephew? You were the only family he had. It was so cruel. You're cruel. He could've helped me. Jeremiah was right. Everything that he said to you was true. That is what Dr Burnside says, and you spoiled it all. You stole his dreams, you stole everybody's dreams. You've turned this place grey and ruined lives and I hate you!'

Sade jumps down from her bed and storms out of her bedroom. She doesn't care if that thing follows her. He may have been a man once; a man that said and did terrible things but the creature he has become is no match for her. The dream he showed her: Jeremiah's dream has made everything clear. The fire transformed Uncle Ezra, changed him into the Dream Thief. That is why his skin is melted and the reason they never found his body.

She saw Jeremiah run off, but that was the end of the dream. Uncle Ezra must have found him and stolen his dreams after the fire. Dr Jeremiah Dean has to be out there still living in The Grey. There is a chance she can save him and he can save her mum and Zach too.

She marches downstairs in her pyjamas, pulls on her wellies and a raincoat from the hook. She grabs a torch from the side and stomps out of the house, across the street and along the side alley of Uncle Ezra's house. She pushes her way through the derelict burnt out house and down the cellar steps. The lights bounce up in joyous greeting and she tells herself not to be afraid of their magic. They are stolen dreams, she thinks, stolen dreams that don't belong to Uncle Ezra. She must be brave and let them go.

She takes the nearest one, a small jar with a greenish hue that throbs gently and quietly at the bottom of its prison. The glass is slightly warm to the touch. She turns the lid, which is stiff at first but then gives way. It takes two or three turns until the lid is off. The dream waits a moment or two, doubting its freedom, then shoots up and out of the jar like a rocket. The power knocks her back a few steps.

The whitewashed walls of the cellar are suddenly flooded with a bright emerald green. Cascades of light shimmer. Sade is filled with a rush of pure pleasure as the dream flies through her, up the chute and out into the night.

Being hit by the emerald dream knocks her once again. She staggers back a few more paces. She flings out an arm to try and steady herself. Floundering about she crashes against a whole shelf of dreams behind her. There's a wobble and anticipating what will happen next, she runs to the safety of the cellar steps still clutching the empty jar in her hands.

She watches the wobble of the jars turn into a dramatic crash as the shelves fall backwards into another stack of shelves behind it. She stares, knowing she can do nothing to stop it, as both shelving units fall back, wedging themselves against one another and the wall. The jarred dreams they were holding slip off and smash onto the stone floor.

The noise is beyond deafening. She screams, drops

the jar she's holding and covers her ears with her hands. The cacophony is not just from the breaking glass, but the dreams themselves; they whizz and pop and bang and fizz like fireworks as they are released from their prisons. The air of the cellar fills with a sudden rush of colours that dance and swirl together, mixing and spitting and crackling as they fight for their turn to escape out of the chute. The performance is magical and Sade, still covering her ears, watches completely spellbound. If only she could keep it, she thinks, and play it over and over again.

The magic that fills the cellar is gone almost as suddenly as it appears. The dust begins to settle like coloured chalks in the air, giving the occasional dying spark and spit like a fire burning down.

She is left staring at the shelves of remaining jars, an ecstatic smile spreading across her face. More, she thinks, I'm going to release them all.

She knows that somewhere in amongst all the jars must be the rest of Jeremiah's dreams. Once she has let them go Sade knows that Dr Jeremiah Dean, like all the people of Stanbridge, will be finally free of The Grey.

She gets to work and grabs the nearest jar. The glass, like the emerald dream before, is slightly warm to the touch. This jar is filled with shimmering gold and silver that swirls within its prison like a sandstorm of precious jewels. It is revved up and anxious to be released like a racehorse at the starting line.

As she begins to turn the lid she remembers the shepherd from Zach's book. She thinks about his feeling of pure happiness when the Dream Eater Demon finally dies. That is the rush she feels when the dreams are released.

As she watches the released dream swirl effortlessly around the cellar and up the chute like a dancer, she wonders where it is going. She wonders if the child that it was stolen from is now grown up and whether they will burst into colour like a flower beginning to bloom.

CHAPTER TWENTY-FIVE

Dream Thief

The Dream Thief hears Sade shout, but she is right, he is weak, too weak to move or answer her. He feels winded and bruised. The dream has bullied and bashed him into nothing. All he can do is stay where he fell and be still.

In contrast to his motionless body, his thoughts twist and collide together, spinning the Dream Thief into turmoil. He was once a man. He saw himself as the real person he once was; a living, breathing man. The Dream Thief watched himself walk and talk with a real human body. He was right there within Sade's dream.

He thinks about the picture on the front of the book and wonders what it is that he has become. Is he a ghoul, a demon? He is nothing real, nor solid, he is nothing more than smoke and magic.

As he lies there, the Dream Thief begins to remember what it was like to be real. He recalls what it was to feel. Memories of his passion and his fight for the things he believed in are awakened. There were other things in his life that gave him pleasure;

he didn't always steal dreams. He begins to see how obsessed he has become. It is an obsession that has destroyed him. It has mutated him into this thing, this grotesque creature that is far from human: a ghoul, a ghost of a man that is feared and loathed.

He hears Sade slam her front door. The Dream Thief knows that he should get up and try to protect his dreams. She is so angry she could do anything; he needs to try to explain, to get her to understand his reasons. If Sade could just see how stealing dreams helps people then maybe they could work together and he would not need to be alone anymore. She could help to control his obsession. Together they could find a way to restore him back to being real. They could help one another.

He tries to sit up but his head is too heavy and fizzes with pain. He wishes he could just sleep deeply again, like he did at the oak tree. That was how he always slept when he was human.

He manages to turn himself gently round, letting the empty jar tumble onto the carpet. He lies flat out on his back. He slowly opens his eyes and sees the huge yellow sun that Sade has painted on her ceiling.

Looking up, he remembers how it felt to have the sun warm his skin. He would like to feel that again. Just as he is thinking of this, the Dream Thief gets the smallest sensation in his right index finger.

It is the tiniest of tingles as if he has been sitting on his hand and the blood is only just returning. He raises his right arm and brings his finger up to his face, astonished. He turns his hand round so that he can look at his tingling finger from all angles. The blackened claw curves menacingly over the tip of his finger. He cannot remember the last time he felt anything real, yet there is definitely a distinct fizzing right at the very tip.

He is still examining his finger, twisting it round every which way, when the real feeling hits. A dramatic surge of pure power barges into his chest like the electric plates doctors use to restart a dead heart.

POW!

It thumps him squarely in the heart.

His heart immediately responds. There is a sudden and dramatic pumping as it catapults back into action. Having lain dormant for decades, his heart beats erratically and fiercely, bursting into life so strongly it feels as if it might power right through his chest.

He gasps at the air around him, pulling in a huge lungful and then another. Oxygen! There is an immediate need for oxygen from his galvanised heart.

His chest swells and broadens to receive the air. His lungs fill and expand like an old, dusty pair of bellows being reawakened after a long, hot summer.

The energised, pumped blood of the Dream Thief begins rushing through tired and disused veins and arteries. It forces its way through dust-filled pathways and down the corridors of his body that have withered away.

Like a dried river coming back to life after years of drought, all of his fresh blood pulses and pushes through him, bringing with it new growth.

The Dream Thief lies on his back panting like a

dog as he grows ever more human. His old ghost-like body dies away being replaced by something more solid. More real.

Like a garden in spring sunshine, all kinds of new life begins to rise up within him. Lost sensations return into his solidifying body. There are no spasms or contortions. Instead he closes his eyes, steadies his breathing and accepts the feeling of warmth that spreads throughout his changing body.

He feels the life-giving blood from his fingers; claws retracting into human fingernails, right down to the ends of his toes, real, human toes. He feels himself grow too, his body taking shape away from the smoke-like wisp of a ghost to a real man, of flesh and bones, with veins and organs, skin that has hair and muscles that pulse with blood from a real human heart.

On and on it goes. Oh the energy! The joy of feeling!

When at last the changes seem complete, the Dream Thief opens his eyes and gently begins to sit up. He sees the strong, bare legs of a man jutting out in front of him. Pale and hairy, but real – real legs, his black cloak way up his thighs.

He brings his hands in front of his body, turns them palms up and over, studies the real fingernails, the human skin. He takes his fingertips to his face, feeling the familiar nose, his full lips, and his broad forehead. He feels the back of his head; he even has his hair back! He laughs, a little burst of pleasure and the noise is real, it is human.

Slowly the Dream Thief stands. Like a new-born foal he is weak and wobbly at first, but after a few slow steps the old memories of how to move like a man begin to return. He practises walking around Sade's room. He does a circuit, passing the flamingos and the lazy leopard.

He goes to the door, turns the handle and walks as softly as he is able across the landing, carefully opening the door to Sade's dad's bedroom. He peers into the room before he enters, but luckily her dad is still sleeping, unaffected by the night's events. The Dream Thief sneaks across the room and softly opens the wardrobe. He helps himself to a pair of jeans, a T-shirt and a jumper and backs out of the room carefully pulling the door closed behind him.

On the landing, he slips out of the tiny black cloak and the ripped clothes underneath and pulls on the new outfit. He keeps hold of his old clothes: he may need proof.

Sade is unlikely to believe what has just happened, especially as he can barely believe it himself.

Now that he is human again she will be able to see the importance of his cause. She will understand his reasons for the things he has done.

CHAPTER TWENTY-SIX

Sade

It's exhilarating, letting the dreams go. She unscrews each jar, reading the label if it's there and waits for the rush of magic. She giggles and throws her arms about, dancing with the colours as the dreams soar about her and away. Sometimes she offers a few encouraging words: 'Go little dream, fly home!'

She wants to find the rest of Jeremiah's dreams; because she knows when she releases them, he will miraculously appear. She's so busy with her task that she doesn't notice the shadow of a man standing on the cellar steps watching her. It is only when he speaks that she stops and turns.

'Having fun are you, Sade?'

She sees the very person she has been expecting. There's no mistaking that funny floppy brown hair and handsome face from her dream. She gives him a huge grin. He's real and free from The Grey: her plan must be working.

'Jeremiah Dean,' she says, and throws her arms wide as if she may just run over and embrace him like an old friend. 'I must have let all your dreams go already. I hoped you would come.'

She lets another dream go, a beautiful silver shimmer dances against the walls like glitter.

'Watch out for your Uncle Ezra though,' she warns over her shoulder, 'he's this horrible ghoul thing that steals people's dreams. He kept them all here in jars.' She waves the lid in her hand at the hundreds of dancing lights still left jostling against their glass, anxious to be released. 'But I'm letting them go.' She's triumphant. 'He stole your dreams, didn't he?' She turns to look at Jeremiah. 'Right after he set fire to all your work? He burnt down your home. I saw it, I saw it all.'

She pauses, but he says nothing. Jeremiah looks different than in her dream. He is older, she decides, but that's understandable. The dream must've been from when he was much younger. Sade notices that he's carrying something. 'What's that in your hand?' she asks.

Sade watches Jeremiah look down at his hand, but before he can answer she speaks again.

'Are you wearing my dad's clothes?' She recognises the faded red V-neck that her dad used to wear a lot. How strange, why on earth would he be wearing her dad's clothes?

'Are those his boots?'

'Um, yes…yes,' says Jeremiah. His voice hesitant, unused and croaky. 'I'm just borrowing them until I can get some. I hope that's okay?'

'But where are your clothes then?' asks Sade still

waving the empty jar around. 'Do they disappear when The Grey goes? That could be embarrassing!' Even as she asks this, she wonders why he would be near her dad's wardrobe when he was lifted out of The Grey. None of this was making much sense to her.

'Um, no they don't disappear; at least I don't think so.' Jeremiah lifts up his hand that clutches something black. Sade recognises it as the cloak of the Dream Thief. 'My clothes are right here, in my hand…only they're a bit small for me now.'

'But isn't that the Dream Thief's cloak?'

'Yes,' says Jeremiah simply.

Sade waits for more, but Jeremiah just stands there looking at her. They stare at one another and Jeremiah's arm that had raised the cloak into the air begins to slowly lower back to his side.

The puzzle pieces begin to slot together in Sade's mind. She realises why Jeremiah has the cloak, why he claims it is his and why he was near to her dad's wardrobe. Her arms drop down heavily beside her. She lets the empty jar fall to the cellar floor where it rolls away, joining the mess of broken glass that surrounds her.

'You're the Dream Thief?' she says, her mouth hanging open in astonishment.

Jeremiah nods.

'But what about the dream that I saw,' says Sade 'that doesn't make any sense.'

'It wasn't a dream; it was a memory,' explains Jeremiah. 'I came to steal your dream, the jar was always empty.' He shows her the empty jar in his hand.

'But what about your uncle? I thought he was the Dream Thief? He was the one who destroyed everything.'

'Uncle Ezra died in the fire,' says Jeremiah, 'I tried to save him, but he'd gone mad. There was nothing I could do. My dreams died with him.'

'So, you're the Dream Thief,' she says, trying to convince herself, 'but you're not, because you're a person.' She looks straight at Jeremiah. 'You look the same as you did in my dream, only a bit older.'

'See, that's the thing,' says Jeremiah, shrugging his shoulders, 'it seems I've become human again. I don't really know how or why, but it feels good to be back. I feel stronger than I have for many years. I feel alive!'

There's a pause and Sade tries hard to make sense of everything.

'Look, I can walk,' Jeremiah hops from one foot to another skipping a bit up and down the cellar steps, 'and talk just like before.'

Sade watches Jeremiah, this man that she had longed to see, dancing around like a puppet. 'What happened?'

'Right after you ran out of your house, an amazing rush of power hit me here.' He pounds the empty jar against his chest. 'It changed me back to being Jeremiah. I had to borrow your dad's clothes, but don't worry he's still asleep, he slept through it all.'

'I don't understand,' says Sade shaking her head. 'You're the Dream Thief? But why would you do such a horrible thing? Jeremiah wanted to heal people. He was a doctor. Zach says he was a miracle worker. Why would you steal dreams?'

The smile fades from his face. 'I know I went too far. It was addictive, the feeling I got. I can see that it changed me.' His voice raises a beat. 'The world is a better place without dreams. When there are no dreams, there's no pain.'

'How can you say that? Look what you did to yourself and to the world around you. You took away the colour, you stole all the life and the happiness away.'

'I have taken away the pain, the fear and the disappointment.'

Sade shakes her head vigorously and her curls bounce in defiance. 'You can't take away people's spirit; you can't break their souls. You're no better than that Dream Eater creature in the book.'

'But I help people,' Jeremiah pleads. 'I make things simple and calm. I protect people from themselves: I stop the pain.'

'There's pain in The Grey, you must see that?' says Sade. 'To live without hopes, without dreams, that's not living it's just…nothing. We need our dreams to be happy and to laugh. Without dreams there's no life.'

Jeremiah sighs and sits down on the bottom step of the cellar, stretching his feet out in front of him. He looks across at the remaining shelves of jarred dreams, straining against their glass prisons. 'You see that jar there?'

Sade turns to look where he points. There's a

large jar, half full of a deep navy blue dream that jitters against the glass like an angry wasp.

'Yeah,' says Sade nodding.

'That was my first dream,' explains Jeremiah. 'I'd been hiding out in people's back gardens waiting for the emergency services to clear out from the house. I didn't know where to go or what to do. I was frightened that they would think I had started the fire and not saved my uncle, so I hid.'

Sade thinks of the boy in her dream, running for his life from the blazing house.

'I was eating the apples off the tree in the garden where I was sleeping when I heard the first ever call of a dream.'

'You heard it?'

Jeremiah nods. 'It was a beautiful piece of music that was played over and over. Each note was so perfectly exquisite I was pulled towards it. Without even thinking I had climbed up onto the garage roof and was peering through the upstairs bedroom window.'

'Was there someone asleep inside?'

'Yes, a young girl. She had dark curls that fanned around her pillow and the beautiful unknown noise was coming from her.'

'What did you do?'

'I watched her sleep, she was restless, but I had this need to get closer. It was not just that I wanted to – I had to see inside the music. I needed to understand how she was doing it, because her lips weren't moving and there was no music playing in her room. It was coming from deep within her and I had to know.'

'Go on.'

'I shimmied up the window, and climbed inside. I still had the empty jar that Uncle Ezra had thrown at me and I carried it inside the house. As I stood next to her my breathing went in and out exactly the same as hers and in that moment I was inside her dream. I could see and hear everything.'

'What was it like?'

'It was magical. I remember the dream. She was painting things that came alive. She painted a multi-coloured horse and was riding it with her paintbrush outstretched. As they galloped along she painted mountains and fields, seas and bridges for her to fly past.'

'Sounds amazing,' says Sade, imagining it in her own mind.

'It was, but then it changed. The girl turned the horse back towards me and stopped. She had seen me: I was the unexpected intruder. She screamed and the horse reared. She began galloping away. I ran after her, I wanted to explain, but she was frightened and I felt the whole mood of the dream change. The sky darkened and the beautiful things she had painted began to wither away and die.'

'Horrible.'

'No, because it was at that moment I felt this most amazing sensation of power. A huge rush to all my senses, I was inexplicably happy. Deliriously happy, despite the dream darkening, despite having my own dreams taken, despite losing my parents and my uncle. In spite of all of these terrible things I was lifted high on a rush of immense power.'

The look on Jeremiah's face is rapturous as he relives the moment.

'Up and up I went and it was then that I remembered the jar in my hand. If only I could keep the feeling and hold onto it, I thought as I opened the lid. Then the dream simply fell from me and into the jar. Thinking I was still inside the girl's dream I screwed up the jar then looked around me.'

'Where were you?'

'Back in the girl's room. The feeling was gone, but when I looked at the jar, I could see it still there. This amazing dancing dark blue light that glowed back out at me. I looked back at the child who slept so peacefully. She was much more restful and I knew that I had helped her. I had taken away all that horrible fear and pain.'

Sade snorts at this, fear and pain that he had caused by invading her dream, she thinks. 'What did you do then?'

'I left her room and walked back to my uncle's house, amazed by what had just happened. I knew then that I could still help people and that is what I have done ever since.'

Sade is stunned. 'Who was the girl?' she asks, even though she knows the answer.

'I never got her name and I regretted it, especially when I realised many years later that I hadn't tightened the lid properly and the dream had been escaping little by little. After that, I went through a phase of always trying to find out the child's name and age. I'd label the jars so as to try and remember, but I forgot nonetheless, so I stopped.'

'I know her name,' Sade snaps, 'she's called Maggie Farrant. She's an art teacher at Stanbridge High. Her life has been ruined by what you did.'

Jeremiah shakes his head. 'No, I helped her, she was so peaceful afterwards.'

'You didn't help her Jeremiah. Why can't you see?'

'She was frightened...'

'Yeah, because of you.'

Sade sighs. He may have been some kind of child genius but he's being pretty thick right now. She tries spelling it out.

'Maggie's dream seeped out from the jar that you didn't tighten properly and went back to her. As it did little thoughts and memories and feelings came back, but she's still not free of The Grey. She needs all of her dream back to heal properly.'

Sade takes Maggie's dream off the shelf in front of her.

'You can make this better. You can undo the damage.'

'There is no damage. Stanbridge is calm, free of pain.'

'Stanbridge is creepy,' she shouts.

Jeremiah bites at the sides of his cheek and picks a bit at the clothes beside him.

She softens. 'You need to help me now to make it better. Look at what has happened to you. Since I smashed all the jars, you're a person again. The power you felt that changed you back into a human, that was the magic from the dreams, dreams that you stole. You said it yourself: you feel so much better now that you're human and not some horrible demon creature. You need to help others to feel better too, Jeremiah.'

He puts his face in his hands and Sade can see him struggle with his thoughts and emotions. She can't wait for him and his conscience. She goes back to the jar in her hands and begins turning the lid. Maggie's dream flips over in ever decreasing somersaults until the lid is off and it shoots up and out of the jar. The cellar becomes a floodlit blue with midnight stars as decoration. The lights rush off up the chute.

'See?' Sade's grin is wide. 'You'll feel as much of a buzz from letting them go, trust me.'

She moves onto the next jar. This time she sees Jeremiah is up and beside her. She sees the trace of a smile pulling at his lips.

He picks up a jar of purples and pinks and raises it up like it is a glass that he will drink from. 'Here's to Sade,' he says, 'the girl who makes you see things differently.' And with his human hands he twists off the lid and releases the dream, plunging the world into a kaleidoscope of colour.

Epiloghe

Sade wakes to a brightness shining down onto her bed. She thinks at first that it's the electric light reflected somehow from her painted sun until she remembers that the horror of The Grey is long gone. The light is real sunshine that streams like honey through her window. She leaps out of her bed as eagerly as Christmas morning and flings open her curtains. The sky is a beautiful, layered bright blue, broken only with the odd cotton wool cloud.

She skips round to her dad's room but he's already out of bed. She finds him downstairs in the kitchen. There's pop music coming from the radio and the whole place is filled with the irresistible smell of frying bacon.

'Good morning, Sah,' he says, 'I'm bunking off work today.' He flips the bacon into the buttered butties and looks up with her with a smile.

'Why?' She takes the plate from her dad and sits down at the table.

'Going to paint the house,' he says joining her.
'Really?'

'Yeah, I hate this grey. I thought we'd go green in here and blue in the downstairs loo. Not sure about the spare room yet, but it's where your mum's going to be so I need it to be right.'

'Well then that's simple,' she says, 'you have to paint it yellow, her favourite.'

She bites into her butty and grins up at her dad.

'Yellow it is then. I can't believe she's coming home.'

'I told you that Dr Dean is a miracle worker, just look how he's helped Zach.'

'Well, he's certainly a good addition to the team up there and Dr Burnside seems very pleased to be working with him.' Her dad takes a bite of his sandwich. 'God knows what research experiments they do down there in the basement but it's got the whole hospital excited.'

'She knows Dr Dean from another time.' Sade chews thoughtfully. 'I think they work well together and now that they've agreed that Mum can come home, I know she'll wake up, she has to.'

'Well I don't doubt that, not now, but it's weird; it feels as if I've been asleep for a long time and I'm only just waking up myself.'

'It's just been hard, that's all, Dad, with Mum sick and everything, but things will be better now.' She finishes her butty.

'How did you get so grown-up all of a sudden? Just how long have I been sleeping?' He smiles at her.

She puts her empty plate in the dishwasher. 'Well,

I need to get dressed and get to school. I can give you a hand with the painting once I get home. Cool?'

'Cool bananas!'

She rolls her eyes as she smiles. 'Oh, Dad!'

Sade starts down her path on her way to school. She waits for two cars and a cyclist, then crosses the street.

'Hello there,' she says, giving a friendly wave to the builders who are busy renovating the condemned house opposite.

'How do,' says one of the builders, tipping his bright orange hard hat.

She walks on down Camberley Street, admiring some of the gardens just coming into bloom. She almost makes it to the end of her street before she hears her name being called out. She looks up to see some kids from her school waving at her. She smiles and waves back.

As she makes her way to Stanbridge High, she watches some of the groups of children walking to school together. Some are swinging their bags or running ahead with their coats on their foreheads like capes. Some are laughing and chatting together easily, or swapping food from their packed lunches.

In the playground a ball is being kicked around by some year-eights and there are girls from different years hanging around the corners of buildings gossiping and laughing. She makes her way towards the entrance, smiling a little to herself and swinging her coat that hangs from her hand.

'Good morning!'

Sade turns to see Maggie smiling at her. Her teacher is wearing a bright striped, full-length cotton skirt and a shocking pink blouse with sort of flyaway sleeves. Different coloured ribbons are threaded throughout her curly, thick, almost black hair.

'Morning, Ms Farrant.'

'How's your mother?'

'Oh much better, thanks. She should be coming home this week.'

'That's fantastic news, you must be thrilled. I hear Zach is doing well too?'

Sade nods. 'Dr Burnside says he's responding really well to the new treatment that Dr Dean has given him and he may even be out of hospital within a week.'

'I bet Seb is pleased.'

'I don't know about that,' says Seb who has snuck up behind them, 'I'll have to move all my stuff and tidy up our bedroom.'

Ms Farrant smiles then checks her watch. 'Off you go, time for registration,' she says then as they hurry away she calls after them, 'I'll see you in class, I've opened up the cupboard, you can paint your dreams, make them colourful.'

'We will,' calls Sade across the playground and she smiles at her teacher as brightly as the sun.

About the Author: Camilla Chester

I've written an entire book; how can a few lines about myself be so difficult? I keep reading lots of 'About The Author' pieces in loads of different books, to get ideas.

Some are dry:

Camilla grew up in Norwich but now lives in Hertfordshire with her husband Ade and their two girls, Fay and Sasha. As well as writing children's fiction Camilla has a small dog walking business. Jarred Dreams is Camilla's debut novel.

Some are silly:

When I was little I thought, 'when I grow up I can eat all the candy floss I want and go on tonnes of roller-coaster rides'. Now I am grown-up I don't want to do that anymore because I know I'd be sick.

Some are somewhere in between:

I wrote this book because I wanted to tell a good story to share with my kids and then, if they liked it, share it with lots of other kids. Writing stories is one of my best things to do, but I also love animals (mainly furry ones that like a cuddle), being with my

friends and family, eating yummy stuff, being outside
in good weather, being cosy inside in bad weather and
anything that makes you go, 'WOW!'

I suppose all three of those might do, but if you want to find out more you can contact me through my website: www.camillachester.com and ask any question you want!

Hip Hip Hoorays

I often think of a baddie first and then the story develops from there. I thought up The Dream Thief with my two girls when we were on holiday. I jotted all the ideas down about the grim and dark world he'd created whilst sitting in the glorious Spanish sunshine! It isn't just Fay and Sasha I need to thank, my husband, Ade, helped too, especially when it came to making the plot plausible.

I want to thank all the writing support I have from my Facebook group, the VWC, SCBWI, the KX Critterati (especially Annie) and all my readers of the many drafts.

The last thanks go to Andy Hunt for his incredible artistic talents and Maxine McCoy for her tireless support and amazing eye for rogue apostrophes.

Thanks Everyone – now for book two, *EATS*:

When best mates Lucas and Tucker win a competition to cook with celebrity chefs everything comes to a boil. Can they stir up trouble and serve the just desserts in time?

Camilla's second book *EATS* is out now.
For more information go to her website:
www.camillachester.com